Throw the Hissy

An April May Snow

Southern Paranormal Fiction Thriller

By

M. Scott Swanson

April May Snow Titles

Foolish Aspirations
Foolish Beliefs
Foolish Cravings
Foolish Desires
Foolish Expectations
Foolish Fantasies

Seven Title Prequel Series

Throw the Bouquet

Throw the Cap

Throw the Dice

Throw the Elbow

Throw the Fastball

Throw the Gauntlet

Throw the Hissy

Never miss an April May Snow release.

Join the reader's club!

www.mscottswanson.com

Author's Note—This is a work of fiction. Character names, businesses, locations, crime incidents, and hauntings are purely imagination. Where the public names of locations are used, please know it is from a place of love and respect from this author. Any resemblance to actual people living or dead or to private events or establishments is entirely coincidental.

"And all those things I didn't say
Wrecking balls inside my brain
I will scream them loud tonight
Can you hear my voice?"

Rachel Platten – "Fight Song"

Chapter 1

"You officially don't have to sleep on the floor."

Dusty's voice draws my attention away from the snarled rat's nest of cords I'm attempting to untangle from the back of my TV. With a quick flourish, he tosses his Phillips-head screwdriver into the air, catches it, and shoves it in his tool belt.

"My hero," I say.

"Happy to help out, ma'am." His John Wayne impersonation leaves a lot to be desired. "Do you need help with that pile of snakes you're dealing with?"

"I need a snake charmer," I say as I turn my attention back to the mess I created.

He stands behind me and watches over my shoulder. "So would you like me to help, or has this become a personal vendetta on your part?"

I huff and hand my older brother the wad of electronic cords. "I don't have the patience for these things."

"You said it, not me," Dusty says as he happily goes to work untangling the wires.

I'm sure I could have hooked up my TV without any assistance —with the right motivation. But it would have taken several days without entertainment before I'd have been sufficiently motivated to set up my equipment. It would take me an hour or two to make the connections correctly. Dusty will have everything working in less than ten minutes.

I don't mind taking advantage of his help while he's here. Besides, he owes me big time.

Last weekend, he blackmailed me into going to a Renaissance fair. I held up my end of the bargain. His part was to help me move from Tuscaloosa to my new apartment in Atlanta, Georgia.

It would be easy to believe I had the better part of the bargain. For the first day of the Renaissance fair, I would have agreed with you. No, I'm not a super geek like my brother, but I do like fantasy and cosplay in moderation. Plus, I'm a huge Tolkien and Rowling fan, so I only made it seem like Dusty was bending my arm when he asked so I could maximize my payoff.

What wasn't fun at the event was when a crazed businessman tried to throw me off a four-story castle wall to make it appear like I had committed suicide. Oh, and then the fact Dusty got himself killed during a jousting competition. Between the two traumatizing events, Dusty dying while I held him has left a much deeper scar. It's the first time in ages I felt fortunate I have paranormal "gifts." If it weren't for my ability to heal, a skill I still don't understand, Dusty would have died in the mud Sunday.

Instead, my red-haired giant of a brother is happily making multiple connections to the back of my TV as if he were a trained technician. I can't describe how happy that makes me.

It occurred to me to tell him he was dead for a hot minute Sunday. But one of two things will come from me telling him he was a goner. Dusty will either laugh it off and say I'm full of baloney, or he would believe me and act like he owes me for the rest of our lives.

I don't want that awkwardness between us.

Dusty stands back and points the clicker at the TV. The news turns on, and he looks at me with his mouth opened wide. "Oh no, we loaded someone else's TV into the van."

"No, we didn't."

"It's set to the news."

I flash him my best 'you're such a dork' stare. "I keep up with the news."

He tosses the remote onto the sofa. "You're just full of surprises. I guess that education really went to your head."

"At least somebody got smarter from their advanced degree."

He grins and ignores me as he surveys my apartment. "I think that about does it."

An unexpected sense of anxiety tidal waves over me. Logically, I know Dusty must go home. For the last seven years, I worked my way through the University of Alabama, earning a business degree and a law degree. I always knew I would one day live alone in my apartment in Atlanta. But now, I feel terribly isolated and anxious.

Dusty's gaze narrows. "You know, I forgot about the cupboards. We still need to go grocery shopping."

"We do?"

"Of course, we do. You must have something to eat before you go to work tomorrow and I'm hungry. You should show your brother some appreciation for helping you move by cooking me something to eat. You don't want me to go to the airport hungry, do you?"

"You know I can't cook." It's shameful but true.

"Still?" He looks shocked. "I mean, that's fine—well, not really. Eating frozen dinners or fast food gets old after a while."

He has a point. That's been my routine for the last few years. I do sometimes miss home for the meals if nothing else.

Dusty gestures toward the door. "Come on. Drive me to the store, and the least I can do is show you how to make mushroom marinara. You can use it for spaghetti, baked ziti, or if you're into the vegan thing like Mom, portobello lasagna."

"What about your plane flight?"

"Don't you worry about that. I can call and change to a different flight. You need to get in your car because we have an important mission to complete before I can leave."

Yes, he's bossing me around like both my older brothers always have. But my mouth is already watering like Pavlov's dog, and the idea of being able to provide a home-cooked meal for myself seems like an excellent survival technique.

An hour later, when we finish unloading all the groceries out of my car, I'm exhausted. Dusty urged me to buy all manner of items I have little confidence I'll ever use. Flour and baking soda? Besides using baking soda, if I run out of toothpaste, who uses either of those items?

He insisted I let him buy my first grocery run. After I objected, I quickly realized any arguments I posed were an act of futility. Dusty is loaded from his *Haunted Haunts* best-selling series of non-fiction books. So, my objection was based on principle and not his ability to pay.

But he filled my buggy with a bunch of useless stuff I'll let sit in my pantry until the expiration date passes. If it made him feel good, who was I to complain if he paid?

He sets two pots on the small economy stovetop. "Okay, both of these are called stockpots. This one with the black lining is the one you use for your sauces, and this metal one you use for your noodles."

I snort a laugh. "Dusty, I know what they are and which ones are for what. I just don't do the cooking part."

He holds a hand up toward me. "A good instructor starts with the basics. Besides, if you do it vice versa, you'll end up with scorched sauce if you're not careful. Nothing is worse than a full pot of beautiful marinara ending up black on the bottom."

I lean against the counter next to him. "Yes, sensei."

Dusty appears to get a kick out of my sass. He pours some olive oil into the Teflon stockpot as well as a tablespoon of minced garlic. "So, you want to swirl the oil and keep the garlic moving until you see it puff into little white balls. You can let them brown a little, but if you're not careful, they'll get too dark really quick."

The smell of toasting garlic takes me back to when I was a little girl watching Mama do her famous lasagna before she took it vegan. I loved the aromas of garlic, olive oil, and tomato. It was a treat for me to watch her put together the many layers of the casserole dishes.

Lasagna night was always a near-religious event. It ranked just behind Thanksgiving, Easter, and Christmas dinner. It might be blasphemous, but most Snows would say they prefer lasagna night.

It is never a meal shared just by our immediate family. My grandmothers and uncles, and often friends of the family, are invited. Mama's recipe makes four full four-quart casserole dishes. And she always says she doesn't want any of it to go to waste.

Everyone knows that's just silly. It wouldn't go to waste, and lasagna always tastes better after it sits for a day.

For as long as I can remember, I have been awed by my mama's beauty. When she cooks her lasagna, a meal she is passionate about, she is even more beautiful than usual.

I recall one time telling her I couldn't wait to make lasagna myself so I could be as pretty as her. She laughed as she layered more noodles on top of the ricotta cheese. Her words have stuck with me ever since.

"April May, you will always be my foolish girl. If you were any prettier, it would hurt people's eyes to look at you, and besides, you're so clever you will always be able to coax someone to cook lasagna for you."

Twenty years later, her statement can make me happy or sad, just depending on what I want to take from it at the moment. That's a synopsis of Mama's and my relationship. I know I love her, and she loves me, but sometimes it's more complicated than it might need to be.

"Okay, so now we turn the heat down and set the timer for fifteen minutes while we get the water for the noodles boiling."

Dusty has a magnificent pot of marinara bubbling lightly. The aroma is incredible. Unfortunately, I have no idea how he made it, save for toasting a tablespoon of garlic.

Dusty leans back in his chair, resting his hands on his stomach. "It's just hard to beat spaghetti."

I hadn't realized how hungry I'd become while moving my furniture into my new apartment today. Now I have overeaten. "Thank you for cooking."

He lifts one of the remaining pieces of garlic toast and splits it in half. "Next time, you cook for me."

"Granny says hope springs eternal."

"I'd consider you a lost cause if you weren't blood, April. There are too many good cooks in our family for you not to have some skill hidden deep down inside."

I stand and collect his plate with mine. I may not cook, but I'm an excellent bus girl. "The fact there are so many good cooks in the family is exactly why I haven't learned. It's just not necessary."

Until now.

My stomach flips, and I develop an instant case of indigestion as I rinse the plates in the sink. Dusty is right. I'm really on my own now.

Technically I was on my own at the university. But everyone knows there is plenty of support in college for anyone who seeks it out. I'm beginning to realize this real-world thing might be a little more difficult and complicated than I planned.

I'm an intelligent and determined girl. I'm sure I'll find my way just fine.

"Are you coming to the lake house this weekend?" Dusty asks.

Here comes the prerequisite interrogation. "I don't think that'll be possible with it being my first week at work."

"Next week?"

"We'll see." That's the truth of it. I told Mama when I moved to Atlanta, I'd make the drive home at least twice a month. She didn't ask me to. It's the regularity that came to mind when I saw the disappointment on her face. She took exception when I informed her I was not moving home to Guntersville after law school.

Trust me, Medusa can't compete with Mama's "disappointment face."

Dusty brings our empty beer bottles into the kitchen. "Are you excited about tomorrow?"

"Instead of butterflies, I feel like I have a flock of geese in my stomach."

He laughs. "Well, dang. Spaghetti was the wrong meal then. I should have made you something bland, like oatmeal."

"I'm glad you didn't."

"You don't have to be nervous. You're going to be fantabulous and the envy of everyone at the firm."

"That's not a word."

"Envy? Sure, it is."

I roll my eyes. "Fantabulous, you doofus."

"Don't question a writer on vocabulary. It's a losing proposition. Besides, even if it's not a word, it describes you perfectly. The only people who should be nervous are all the other junior lawyers at your new firm. Their hopes of ever making partnership just evaporated."

"All right, it's getting a little deep in here. Don't make me break out my galoshes." As I wipe down the stovetop, I notice the time. "Oh my gosh, is it already nine?"

"Yep. Time gets away from you when you're busy."

"I need to give you a ride to the airport, and I haven't even considered what I'm going to wear tomorrow." The marinara in my stomach feels like it's back in the stockpot bubbling.

"Chill. I'll just order a ride. Besides, I feel better knowing you're here at your apartment rather than on the other side of town in that death trap you call a car."

"No, I need to take you to the airport."

Dusty holds up his left hand, gesturing for me to hush as he pulls out his phone. "This is not up for discussion. I'm not going to allow you to go to your first day with bags under your eyes and wrinkled clothes."

Yes, it makes me feel like a heel that my brother is getting a cab instead of letting me take him to the airport. I'm even more ashamed that I'm grateful I won't have to drive him across town.

I had thrown my wardrobe up as soon as Dusty finished installing the closet's organizing shelves for me. But I have not put any thought into what I'm wearing tomorrow. What I wear to the office in the morning could change the trajectory of my career. Don't scoff. First impressions can be that important, especially for professional women.

"They'll be here in five minutes."

Every muscle in my body tenses. This is it. This is the jumping-off point of no return.

Dusty gestures toward the door. "Stand outside with me until they show up."

I nod in agreement and follow him out. We walk down the sidewalk to where my car is parked.

"Just as a side note before I leave. I know you're about to make mind-boggling money. Still, if you ever need a little extra cash. For an exotic vacation—or I don't know—a car that isn't held together with coat hangers and Bondo, remember, I pay really well for paranormal story leads. Also, I can always use your unique skills during an investigation if you can find the time."

I have been feeling guilty ever since we left the Renaissance fair Sunday. There was a ghost at his friend Gabe's castle, and I never mentioned it to Dusty. I have my reasons. Most of all, trying to remain sane. It's easier on my sanity when I don't have random disembodied voices speaking to me. Still, I realize reporting on the paranormal is how Dusty makes his living.

"I need to tell you something," I say.

"What's that?"

"There was a ghost at Gabe's castle."

He smiles. "I know."

"You saw her?"

"No. But when the paramedics were loading Gary into the ambulance, he mumbled something about a lady in blue. I knew he didn't jump from the turret wall of his own volition.

I also have seen you mad but never angry enough to throw somebody else from a roof." He grimaces. "Actually, the fact you had on a yellow T-shirt had as much to do with convincing me you hadn't hurt him. Since there was no one else on the roof, I figured it was Oana's ghost."

"Yeah," I whisper. "Why didn't you say something?"

"You looked shellshocked, and I'm not going to press you after an event like that." He favors me with a smile. "After you come to peace with the event, might I remind you, I pay really well for paranormal stories."

I laugh. "I'll take that under advisement."

A black SUV stops behind my Prius. A chill causes me to shudder.

"That's my ride."

"Yep." I'm struggling to not get emotional.

Dusty turns and gives me a hug. His mouth is close to my ear, and he whispers, "I'm proud of you, April May. You just do you, and everything will be fine. And if anybody messes with you, just tell them to kiss your grits."

He kisses me on the forehead and drops his arms. "Don't do anything to embarrass the family name."

I snort a laugh. "Of course not."

Opening the SUV door, he says, "Good, because that's Chase's job."

I step off the sidewalk onto the parking lot as the SUV pulls away and continue watching until the brake lights disappear. This just got real.

Chapter 2

Why I even bother to set my alarm, I'm not sure. I might have fallen asleep for an hour at the most. At four thirty, I decide I might as well get up and take a shower.

I'm not due in the office until nine. But I plan on arriving thirty minutes early just in case I have any difficulties on the way to the office.

The interview process with Master, Lloyd, and Johnson was extensive and brutal. It was a battery of ten separate interviews culminating in one final meeting at the Atlanta headquarters. For eight hours, all twelve partners interviewed me individually.

Would I ever want to do it again? Not unless my life depended on it. Still, the size of the carrot they dangled in front of me kept me going strong. The idea of defending the top entrepreneurs, entertainers, and professional ballplayers in Atlanta is tailor-made for my life goals.

I put on a robe and wrap my hair in a towel as I pad to the kitchen for the most important meal of the day. I scan the contents of my refrigerator. Impressive. After a moment of considering the eggs and bacon, I pull down the Cap'n Crunch box stored on top of the fridge.

I'll start eating better tomorrow. But my nerves are shot right now, and some comfort food will calm me down.

Honestly, I have no idea why I'm so keyed up. There were a

thousand applicants for the two positions at Master, Lloyd, and Johnson, and they selected me. That means I must have something special. Right?

If they think I'm special enough to rise to the top, why am I so worried? Because of that little voice in my head that keeps tapping a fingernail on my brain while it says, "Fraud. April is a fraud."

I'm not. I have the degree to prove it, and I know I'm an incredible litigation attorney, if I say so myself.

It's not my education. It's where I'm from that makes me feel like a fraud.

There is no way to know for sure, and I'll find out soon enough, but I imagine most of the lawyers at the firm come from large metropolitan areas. Charlotte, Richmond, Nashville, Jacksonville, and a healthy number of them are homegrown Atlanteans.

Tuscaloosa was a vast city to me when I moved there from Guntersville. I'm not sure if I'll be able to make the jump to the largeness of Atlanta. But I know I want to. I must make this work because it's the only way I will secure the future I have dreamed of since I was a little girl.

I can't let a case of self-doubt sabotage my life goals. I have worked too long and hard for this day.

Rinsing my bowl in the sink, I practice deep breaths and push my shoulders back. *You've got this, April May. You're fantabulous.* Darn it, Dusty. Now I have that stupid word stuck in my head.

I walk to the bathroom to dry my hair and brush my teeth. As I put the paste on my toothbrush, my eyes go to the stylish white skirt and black jacket I selected for my first day. Very professional.

It's the bright yellow pumps I plan to wear that bring a smile to my face. I know some guys believe in power ties. I put my faith in power shoes. Besides, shoes make a much bolder statement. Probably because they're functional. Ties are like an odd male cousin of the scarf, an accessory at best and a nod to the antiquated patriarchal system at worst.

I inspect my makeup for the third time in the last fifteen minutes and check the time. It's only seven a.m. I strategically selected my apartment and should have a short fifteen-minute commute to the MLJ office. Still, my nervous energy level is about to drive me crazy, and I figure it would be best to go on into work. I can always wait in the parking lot until eight thirty for my nine o'clock appointment.

The humidity coats my skin the moment I step outside of my air-conditioned apartment. I can feel my hair curling and my makeup melting off my face as I quickstep to my car. I open the car door and start the engine. Immediately, I direct all the air registers at my face to save my makeup.

No, this isn't anything new. I have lived with this level of humidity all my life. Excuse me if I had hoped for a reprieve on the first day of my new career.

Daddy always says the humidity is excellent for the skin. That's why all Southerners look good at their funeral viewing. Personally, I'd opt for a closed casket if it meant I didn't have to become soaking wet every time I step outside eight months out of the year.

Pulling out of the parking lot, I realize I'm not as early as I think I am. I'm shocked at how backed up the roads are already. Most aggravating, at each red light, the vehicles crossing in front of us have an awful tendency to block the intersection. When our light turns green, we sit and hope the car in front of us can find a seam between the vehicles blocking the intersection.

I'm busy fuming over the rudeness and stupidity of the drivers blocking the intersection and don't notice the flow of traffic slowing in front of me. To my chagrin, my light turns red, and now I'm the rude, stupid jerk blocking traffic.

I look straight ahead and ignore the cacophony of horns blaring at me. Then I lean forward and act as if I'm changing the radio station. They don't know my radio isn't on.

Note to self, when checking drive time from a new apartment to a new job, you should do that during rush hour. Doing it on a Saturday afternoon is pointless.

The traffic thankfully begins to flow well, and we creep up to twenty miles per hour. My GPS indicates I'm less than a quarter-mile from MLJ's headquarters, and an icon for Creative Cupcakes pops up on my screen.

Now that's just dirty pool.

I check the time, and it's seven forty. I have plenty of time to run in, get a cupcake, and if I'm careful, I can eat it in the parking lot of the law firm.

To be extra cautious, I'll lean over my passenger seat. That way, if a piece of frosting breaks off, it won't smear on my outfit. If it were not for the hundred percent humidity, I could just eat my cupcake outside.

As I pull into the Creative Cupcakes parking lot, my phone rings. I grin when I see the ID pop up as "Chase." I turn on my ear-bud. "What's up?" I ask.

"Dusty told me it was your first day. I want to make sure you're doing all right."

"Thanks."

"Did you get a corner office?"

"That might be a few years."

"Geez, Dusty said you were a good negotiator. Just goes to prove he's full of it."

"That's not very supportive of you."

He laughs. "Oh, I'm not worried about you. It's the rest of the firm I'd worry about."

I try not to laugh as I act put out. "So, did you have a reason for calling, Chase, or did you just want to call and harass me as I'm going in for my first day at work?"

"Oh yeah, I meant to ask, have you checked out the fishing at Lake Lanier yet?"

The line moves, and I'm at the ordering speaker. "Hey, hold on a minute." I put Chase on mute as I review the scrumptious menu I already know by heart. Creative Cupcakes has franchises across the entire Southeast.

"Can I help you?" The radio crackles.

"Yes, I'd like a strawberry red velvet and a small coffee, please."

"Second window, please."

I unmute my phone. "I don't have time to go fishing. I just moved in the other night."

"You don't have to get all tense about it. You're not still holding the accident against me, are you?"

The irritation drains quickly from me and is replaced with remorse. I hate it that Chase would even think I'd hold the accident against him. "Of course not, Chase. That was an accident. How many times do I have to tell you this?"

"I don't know. It just seems like you've been avoiding the idea of fishing with me since it happened."

"I have avoided it because I have always tried to beg off fishing trips. It's just not my thing. If it were with anyone other than you, I'd never go."

True story, despite having grown up on one of the best freshwater fishing lakes in the country—you can try to argue that with me, but you won't win. The only reason I go fishing is that I like talking to my brother Chase.

"All right. I'll take you at your word. But to prove it to me, you'll have to give me a date to bring the boat down so that we can go fishing on your lake."

"It's not *my* lake, Chase. Besides, this whole real-world thing might take some time to adjust to. I'm going to be busy for a good while just getting my feet under me."

"Oh, hey, April. I got to go. Bill Carter's coming in, and I need to get his boat in the water."

"Okay."

"Congratulations on your first day. I know you're going to be awesome. I love you."

"I love you, too."

I hang up and can't help but think about what happened four months ago. Chase and I set out early to fish Lake Guntersville. That morning has recently irreparably changed my life into a private nightmare.

The night before we set out to fish, we had severe weather in Guntersville. A massive thunderstorm blew through town, packing straight-line winds clocked at seventy miles per hour. Fortunately, there was only minor tree damage in our neighborhood.

Per our usual schedule for fishing, which is four times a year, Chase packed our breakfast and lunch, and I helped him load the bass boat. We pushed off into the thick fog just as the sun was trying to shine through the gray cloak over the lake's glass-like surface. We'd only been on the water for ten minutes, and we were passing the state campground when we both spotted a dark shadow on the water.

But it was too late.

The log seemed to float up to the surface out of nowhere as we approached. One second it wasn't there. The next, half of an old oak tree lay in our path.

Chase turned the boat hard to the left to steer clear. In retrospect, that was the wrong thing to do. We hit the tree at near top speed at an odd angle that flipped the boat and catapulted both of us through the air.

I don't remember anything before waking up at the hospital that night. Despite several cracked ribs and a concussion, Chase managed to get both of us out of the water.

Other than having been knocked out for an extended period, I was fine. Physically.

The problem is that since the accident, my paranormal abilities, which had atrophied while I was in college and away from Sand Mountain, have come to life and strengthened exponentially. I've experienced more creepy, unexplainable events in the last four months than the previous fifteen years since I first developed my "gifts" at the age of twelve.

Also, my weirdness is back with a vengeance. I have more skills now than I possessed when I was younger, and they're growing exponentially more powerful every day.

Before the accident, my abilities consisted of hearing voices when I was alone. Occasionally, I would see an accompanying translucent figure I took to be a ghost. On rare occasions, when someone was emotionally charged, I could glean visions from their thoughts.

Nana Hirsch taught me how to build partitions in my mind to quiet the voices when I needed them to go away. I became less surprised when I would see an apparition, and I managed to not touch anyone when they were emotional. In short, I learned to manage my skills, and it worked well for me, to the point that most days, I didn't even remember I had the weird abilities.

Since our accident, paranormal activities have been commonplace. It's an oddity when I'm *not* afflicted with them. This is a fact I am less than thrilled about. I have enough balls in the air without having to handle a breakout of the freaky April skill set.

I roll down my window to pay for my cupcake.

"Hi. That'll be nine thirty-four," the middle-aged woman says with a practiced smile lacking in genuineness.

I hand her my card, and she pushes my coffee and cupcake out the window. When she returns my card, I thank her and pull out of the lot.

It's not Chase's fault, but our conversation has knocked some of the shine off my cupcake purchase. It's been a few days since I have had a paranormal event. Something I'm praying will be my new norm. My hope is that if I immerse myself in my legal career and stay away from Sand Mountain and anywhere else with a high level of supernatural activity, my "gifts," as my grandmothers like to call them, will atrophy like they did when I was in Tuscaloosa.

The conversation with Chase only serves to remind me I still don't know why my paranormal abilities are strengthening. It's a mystery only equaled by why they bloomed into existence when I was twelve. Given the option of understanding why the skills grow or being rid of my affliction, I'd choose them to disappear today never to be experienced again.

Chapter 3

The headquarter parking lot is an alcove hidden between majestic pines and large azalea bushes. The well-maintained, three-story bronze metal structure with blue-tinted glass shines like a football championship ring sitting atop a knoll in the middle of a well-kempt forest. That's what the building symbolizes to me, too—my championship payoff from fifteen years of working my plan.

The entire parking lot is packed with vehicles, including three box trucks parked in the fire lane at the front of the building. I circle back around and find a sliver of asphalt next to a Ferrari parked in the middle of two spaces. I squeeze in slowly.

As I turn my car off, fear paralyzes me. I have never had a "real job" before now.

Don't misunderstand. I have worked my entire life and am not afraid of it. My first job was working for Mama at the family marina. But to be fair, it was impossible to get fired, even though I tried every summer. My next job was a bit of a step up. I waited tables in Tuscaloosa as I worked my way through college.

In both cases, they were jobs that if I lost them, would never blemish my résumé. Today marks the line of demarcation between having a job and starting a career. Yes, I prepared relentlessly for this day. I planned for seven long years and ran up student debt that looks more like a mortgage on a modest suburban home.

It's the unknown stoking my doom and gloom intuitions. I'm not in college anymore. There will be no syllabus to tell me what to expect or plan for daily. I must rely on my training and wiles and nothing else to forge my success.

Rachel Platten's "Fight Song" comes to mind, and I began to sing it to myself. My volume increases until I'm grinning like a loon as I belt out the end of the chorus. I take a deep breath, squint my eyes as I set my "game face," and check my reflection in the rearview mirror. "You've got this, April May Snow."

I approach the magnificent building and give thanks for making the LCAT score that allowed me to attend a top-notch law school. The third-year students from Alabama are one of only three schools Master, Lloyd, and Johnson even consider for interviews for their junior associate positions. They also require prospective candidates to be in the top quartile of their class.

I try to be humble, but you'll have to excuse me if I'm proud of the fact I finished in the top ten percent of my class. It took three years of managing on four hours of sleep each night and drinking enough caffeinated beverages to keep a local coffee shop open. Still, I earned my ranking, and it was integral to me landing one of the two positions Master, Lloyd, and Johnson filled this year.

Why is it such a big deal to get a position with MLJ? Money. The firm negotiates, contracts, and delivers some of the best business acquisitions in the Southeast. Purchases that allow their largest holding firm to keep the earnings churning continually.

Besides, their client list includes the top executives, entertainers, and professional sports figures of the Atlanta market. MLJ is the preferred firm for handling high-profile clients' inconvenient "personal" legal issues and doing it with the utmost discretion.

Understand, I did my part in college. I protested. I held recycling drives, food drives and get out the vote drives.

An odd thing happened as my student debt skyrocketed, and

I realized I wasn't just poor; I was majorly in the hole. The only "green" April May Snow cares about *presently* is the kind I can put in the bank and has the heady scent of fresh ink.

If it means I'm forced to break apart some hundred-year-old family-owned business, well, that's not on me. I'll just be doing the paperwork. It was going to happen anyway.

I pull the information pack from my purse, which arrived from human resources three weeks earlier. I know my contact is Jan Miller, but I want to review the information one more time.

Even though Jan is officially my recruiter, I have only met her in person twice. The rest of our interviews have been via Zoom.

As I step up the cut marble stairs, I step aside for two muscle-bound young men in coveralls, carrying a file cabinet strapped to a dolly. One man grips the dolly handles while the other eases the wheels down the stairs by lifting and lowering the file. When I'm parallel with the young man backing down the stairs, his head snaps hard to the right, and his lips part as he commits my shape to memory.

That's right. I clean up nice when I put my mind to it. But I'm not here to impress the movers.

Continuing up the stairs, I pull open the heavy glass door and walk up to the receptionist's desk. It's vacant. I wait. I peek around the dividing wall and peer down a long marble corridor. I consider walking down the hallway to see if I can find assistance before I end up being late on my first day on the job.

"Conference room."

The male voice behind me causes me to jump as my heart stops, and I nearly pee myself. "What?" I ask a little too harshly of the mover who ogled my breasts moments earlier.

"They are all in some big meeting in the conference room."

I need to get to Jan Miller before I'm officially late. "Do you work here?"

"Nah," he says with an easy grin. It's a smile a girl could fall in love with if she had the time to and didn't have to take care of a career first.

"I was hoping you could tell me where I could find Jan Miller's office. I have an appointment to meet her right now."

"So, what's your name, beautiful?"

I can't believe he's chatting me up at such an inopportune time. Admittedly, there is the possibility if your IQ is under eighty, it might seem like a perfect segue into exchanging telephone numbers.

"Beautiful works just fine, sir."

The second mover squints his eyes and smacks the talkative one on the arm. They both glare down the hallway.

I can't stand the suspense anymore and just peek around the wall. Did I mention to you I have an insanely elevated level of curiosity and zero patience?

I'm shocked to see three well-dressed white men being led toward the front door in handcuffs. Each has their head hung low as they look away from the rest of the staff. They're bracketed by men with expressions so grave I step back to give their somber parade room to pass as they approach.

"What's going on?" I whisper to the movers.

"I suppose they did something bad," big, beautiful, and dull surmises.

I can't help myself. "What did you say your name is?"

His easy smile makes another appearance, and I swear my knees unhinge. "Shane."

"Do you have a pen, Shane?" Maybe it's because he sees my chest flushing, but Shane knows why he needs a pen and doesn't miss a beat as he pulls a Sharpie out of his pocket and holds the black tip to the palm of his substantial long-fingered hand.

"It's 256-555-0121," I say at an exaggeratedly slow pace.

His smile broadens. "All right, Bama."

So, he knows area codes. That makes him a good bit smarter than some of the men I have dated.

No, the fact Shane will never set the world on fire in the academic department is not a deterrent. In some ways, when you're looking for someone to spend some time with and not marry, it's a bonus. Besides, from my neck of the woods, the boys come primarily in two flavors—beautiful, sweet, and dumb, or crazy-eyed smart. Crazy-eyed smart boys make the hair on the back of my neck stand up and not in a good way.

The six serious men leading the procession each wear bullet-proof vests and a thin nylon windbreaker. As they pass by us with the three disgraced executives, the acronym FBI in bright yellow on the back of their dark jackets seems to tattoo onto my retinas.

It's the first time it occurs to me something might be amiss at the highbrow firm of Master, Lloyd, and Johnson. The first twinge of anxiety tweaks my stomach, and I feel sick.

"Shane, do you know where the ladies' room is?"

"I believe I saw it down there on the left, Bama. Just before you get to the double doors of the conference room."

"Thank you. Give me a call if you have a mind to."

He smiles and gives a subtle nod. "I might do that, Bama."

Turning, I roll my eyes, thankful his typical male reaction has taken my mind off my bubbling stomach. No matter how in-tellectually challenged they are, all men come out of the womb with the innate ability to play the sexual dance.

I figure I might never hear from the big, beautiful lug. Not be-cause he's not interested, he is, but because his hands will sweat my phone number off within the hour, and he'll have no way of contacting me.

As I reach the ladies' room, I'm beginning to feel better, but I take a stall just in case. As I close the door behind me, I hear mul-tiple sets of heels enter the tiled room.

"I will kill him!" I hear a familiar voice exclaim.

"Calm down, Jan."

"Don't tell me to calm down, Rachel! I have a mortgage and two kids. You've got Tom's income to fall back on. It's easy for you to be calm!"

"You don't have to be so hateful, Jan."

"You're a ditz, Rachel. Do you think those three are just going to take what's coming to them? Let me remind you they enlisted our help on everything. Everything! Our fingerprints are all over those records. Once those three start scratching to find a way to keep their saggy white butts from spending time in a real jail, I guarantee you they'll attempt to make it look like they had some rogue middle managers. Managers who were cooking the books while they were unaware. Don't you get it? They're going to claim they had no idea the company was involved in illegal transactions."

"Jan, you are always so cynical. They wouldn't do that to us."

"Why? They are criminals, Rachel. Can't you get that through your dense skull?"

"Well, I don't believe you. Besides, even if the bosses tried to pin it on me, I followed management's directives."

"Lord, you are a dense woman. Tell me, those little 'bonuses' you received—were they on Master, Lloyd, and Johnson checks?"

There is a pause before Rachel answers. "No, they were always from the holding company."

"Ding, ding, ding. Theoretically, you could have arranged the transfer of the losing acquisitions to the subsidiary holding company."

"Well, I did, but on their directive."

"You know what, forget it. The best advice I can give you is to go home and get your house in order as if you are going on a three-year vacation to a terrible resort."

I stand paralyzed in the stall as the women continue to discuss specifics of the dealings that I'm sure precipitated the raid by the FBI. Details I don't care to hear, and I'm sure an FBI agent would love to have delivered to them on a recording.

It feels like an eternity before the women finally exit the restroom. I cautiously peer out from the stall and confirm I'm alone. With the coast clear, I slip back into the hallway.

The office is alive with professionals in suits and pantsuits scurrying from the building. Everybody has the appearance of needing high blood pressure medication.

I check the time on my phone and see I have precisely three minutes to find Jan Miller. Otherwise, I'm late. I still clutch tightly to the hope that somehow this morning's events will not impact my position at the firm.

Shane comes up the hallway carrying a personal computer, the cords dragging the ground. "You still here, Bama?"

"I still have not located Jan Miller's office."

Shane's perpetual smile melts. My experience with boys like Shane? If they look worried, it's not a tough situation. It's a nightmare. "Bama, she's in the corner office on the right. Maybe you can reschedule for another day?"

A nervous laugh explodes from my mouth. "No. I have an appointment."

Shane favors me a one-shoulder shrug and continues with the computer toward the exit.

I march as quickly as I can on my heels to the end of the hall. The last office door on the right is open, and I knock confidently on the door as I step into the office. Jan is an impressive, tall, auburn-haired woman—her head jerks up to the wrap on the door, her jade eyes narrow as her mouth sets in a fierce snarl. "What?"

"Ms. Miller?" My voice sounds like a squeak to me.

"What?" Her single word oozes venom.

I take that as an invitation and gather my composure. "Ms. Miller, I'm your new hire, April Snow." I stride assertively across her office with my hand extended.

Jan looks at my hand as if I had just dunked it in a vat of chicken guts. "And?"

"Today is my orientation?"

She sighs. "There will be no orientation."

I hope the grin that blooms on my face isn't as idiotic looking as it feels. "Oh, when do we need to reschedule it to?"

"Never."

My stomach clenches tightly. "Excuse me?"

Jan raises her eyebrows and waves her hand in an arcing motion around her office. "Sweetie." The word sounds like an insult when Jan says it. "There is no job. There is no more Master, Lloyd, and Johnson for that matter."

I follow the motion of her hand and notice the discoloration on the wallpaper that would be a perfect outline for six file cabinets. I also see the array of cables leading to the top of her desk plugged into nothing. "Hey, I moved to Atlanta for this job. I declined all the other offers."

"Sucks for you," Jan says with a toss of her auburn mane. "You should count yourself lucky you didn't work here, or you'd be looking at some jail time too, Mary Jo."

"April May," I correct her.

"Whatever. Where do you hicks come up with those dreadful names anyway?"

Up to this point, my world had been spinning out of control in despair—then my attitude catches a gear, and my redneck comes out in full force. "Well, I'd say it's been a pleasure, but I make it a point not to lie, *June*. I wish you the best of luck with your jail time and hope you and your cellmate develop a tight bond. I'll show myself out."

I feel that's a strong comeback, considering Jan's words have just brought my life dreams crashing down around my feet. Planning to stride confidently out of her office, I turn and slam into the doorframe, nearly knocking me onto my butt. The pain is excruciating and feels like someone hit me with a baseball bat.

Awesome. Now I have a huge bruise to go with my bruised ego. Assuming I have not broken my clavicle.

I readjust and stomp out of the office, attempting not to cry from the pain emanating from my shoulder. The ache is helpful at this point. It gives me something to focus on besides the fact my life just ended.

How in the world did I let myself get involved with such terrible people? This is the famed MLJ of such high repute? Three executives being marched out of their offices by the FBI and the rest of the staff scurrying like wild animals trying to escape a forest fire?

How did I not get some read on the level of evil that must reside in the organization? What good are psychic abilities if I can't use them for my own benefit?

I slam into something as solid as a wall and am knocked sideways off my heels. I'm falling and the black marble floor is rushing up fast to meet me when someone grabs me, and I hear a loud crash.

"Whoa, Bama." Shane lifts me up and sets me on my unsteady legs. "Careful there. You don't want to break an arm."

"I do, but not mine," I grumble as he goes to a knee to pick up the computer he dropped to save me.

Shane cuts his eyes up at me. "Are you okay?"

No, no, I'm not. Every cell in my body hurts right now. I can't believe this is happening to me. April May Snow. I have busted my tail my entire life for this moment. This was supposed to be it. This was when I was supposed to get what I deserved, what I earned. Then in one morning, it's blown away by a tornado beyond my control.

"Hey."

A beautiful guy is standing in front of me, looking concerned as if I took a tumble on the marble floor. Why did I even talk to this guy? I should have been laser-focused on my career, today of all days. Typically, I wouldn't have spoken to him, so why now?

I suppose because he is incredibly delicious.

Plus, thirty minutes ago, I felt like I was on top of the world, and power is one powerful aphrodisiac. There is no way to measure it, but if there were, I bet I was the most confident woman in the world for about ten minutes. And you know what? It felt good. Good, like I'm watching my favorite movie, eating homemade strawberry ice cream, and Amazon delivers my new uber-cute pumps. The delivery guy hands me a check for a million dollars because I'm Amazon's quintillionth customer.

Yeah, that sort of good.

"Do you need me to call somebody for you?"

I squint my eyes. "What?"

"Is there someone I can call for you?"

"Why?"

He flashes the sexy smile I don't need as a distraction. "You just look like you need to talk to someone."

I don't need to talk to anyone. I need to get the heck out of this evil place. The tears well in my eyes, and all I can think to do is stride down the hallway with the little bit of dignity I can muster. As I take the first step, Shane reaches out and holds my wrist. I sling his hand off me. "Don't touch me!"

He winces. "My bad."

An odd mixture of emotions roils through me as I stomp toward the tinted glass door. I'm mad enough to spit nails, and at the same time, I'm so sad it's difficult not to spring a leak and start sobbing.

I hit the glass door so hard with my right hand I may have added a sprained wrist to the bruised clavicle. At this rate, I'll be on injured reserve by the time I reach my car.

Chapter 4

I yank open my car door and fall onto the seat. As I wait for the air conditioner to knock the inside temperature down from Death Valley hot to just muggy, I watch Shane exit the building. He's carrying the PC he dropped when I ran into him. The cord is dragging behind him.

Now I can add guilt to the toxic concoction of emotions running through me. Shane was just trying to be thoughtful, and I was beyond rude.

I'll have to forgive myself for that indiscretion. I was under duress. Besides, I'll never see Shane again anyway, and he will forget about me in the next hour.

I'm not sure what my plan is now, but I know I can't stand to sit in this stupid parking lot any longer. I throw my car into reverse and pull out of the parking spot, nearly trading paint with the Ferrari.

The worst part is that this isn't my town, so I don't know where to gather my thoughts. I need a place with water. Bodies of water always calm me.

If I were in Tuscaloosa or Guntersville, I'd know where to go. My car would take me there on autopilot while I ran the terrible events through my mind.

But I don't know this town. So far, all I have seen in Atlanta is a lot of tall buildings and traffic. Nothing here reminds me of Alabama other than the giant pine trees and the oppressive heat.

I pull out of the MLJ parking lot and think good riddance. As Daddy likes to say, things happen for a reason. I'm just hoping the reason is that something better is around the corner. Presently, I'm having a tough time convincing myself of that.

In no time, I'm sitting in traffic again. So far, traffic is my least favorite aspect of Atlanta. Well, after the firm formerly known as Master, Lloyd, and Johnson, of course.

As I sit in traffic staring at the bumper in front of me, it occurs to me. At the same time my psychic abilities failed to warn me about MLJ, I had plenty of warnings from my family. Unfortunately, I chose to ignore Uncle Howard's pet name for the firm, Wee, Cheatham, and Howe. I dismissed his low opinion of my prospective employer as envy of the sour grapes variety.

I should be ashamed of myself. My family always has my best interest in mind. I don't know why, in this instance, I chose to assume they were trying to sabotage my unbelievable opportunity.

I was right about the unbelievable part. There was nothing about the MLJ offer that was legitimate.

Like Jan said, I dodged a bullet by never having worked for them. It'll be difficult enough to get a job on short notice. I can only imagine if I were being investigated for some embezzlement crime.

It sounds like Jan may end up going to jail. Or at least she gave the impression she was concerned about it. I wouldn't wish incarceration on anybody, but my empathy reserves are running on empty. It's my opinion if anybody could use the attitude adjustment of spending time in jail, it's the redheaded witch who goes by the name of Jan Miller. The *former* human resources director of MLJ.

The traffic moves, and I'm not particularly relieved. It means I must pay attention, and I'm so numb, if I were at my apartment, I'd curl up into a ball and sleep for days. As I pass by Creative Cupcakes, I'm not the least bit motivated to pull into the parking lot for another cupcake. I won't have an appetite for a long time.

Shane had the right of it. I need to talk to somebody in the worst way. There is one massive issue with the idea. There is no one I can talk to about today's events.

Martin, my best friend from law school, would understand. Still, I don't want to sound like a failure.

My cousin, Tricia, would undoubtedly want me to call her, but Tricia has always looked up to me. She is currently struggling to work her way through law school. The last thing I want to do is to undermine her ambition. What would it do to her if she thought she wouldn't be able to get immediate employment with a good firm after she earned her Juris doctorate?

My family? Oh, heck no.

After the "we're so proud of you, April" parade they showered on me the last few weeks, I don't know how I call and tell them they were right. That the firm I hitched my wagon to is a criminal organization.

No, I just don't think that's a conversation I care to have any time soon.

That's okay, April. You've been doing things on your own your entire life, and this is just another situation you'll work through. I just need a plan to work.

One plan is to firebomb the MLJ headquarters. That would be an excellent plan. I visualize the glass blown onto the parking lot as fire rolls out from the building. A file cabinet blown into the air has landed on a Ferrari, crushing the hood of the pompous, privileged emblem of snobbery.

That would be worth at least twenty years in prison, assuming nobody is hurt. My smile dissipates.

The scenery has changed. I'm in a residential area. The homes are large, brick, and approaching four thousand square feet. From the overgrown shrubs, crowded large trees, and the dated architect, I take the neighborhood to be from the seventies or early eighties.

The road is wide but winding. I come around a bend in the street, and my Prius goes airborne as I take a speed bump at forty miles an hour.

I fight to control the steering wheel. "Good job, April," I say as

I rub my neck that feels whiplashed.

I'm still checking for loose teeth when I come up to a small playground. It is part of a small elementary school, and I take a right into the vacant lot.

What ticks me off the most about MLJ is I had twenty other offers available to me during my third year of law school. Good firms, not of MLJ stature, but firms I could've made a respectable living working at and not had to deal with today's drama.

It would be one thing if this were the first time MLJ has messed up my plans. But that's hardly the case.

When I graduated from law school seven weeks ago, MLJ informed me they were holding off on my employment until the second student hired could start. Because of somebody I had never met, I was forced to hustle and scrimp for enough money to survive two months while saving my apartment's deposit and first month's rent.

Oh no. I totally forgot about the lease.

Once again, another "I told you so" from my family. Daddy told me to insist on a six-month lease in case I decided I didn't like the apartment I initially selected, or it was unsafe.

I thought he was worrying too much. It was sheer luck to get an apartment at the complex I did. The clientele is exclusively young professionals and exceptionally safe. I assumed it would be a terrific way to meet a few friends and, who knows, even a guy or two who could spark my interest. Yes, I signed a one-year lease.

That'll be fun to pay, with no job.

I'm not totally broke, but four weeks is all the cash reserves I have left. Six weeks if I decide to drop the extra fifteen pounds I'm carrying by not eating.

As I calculate if I can find employment before my money runs out, it is doubtful. It took me ten weeks of interviews to land the job at MLJ, and most of the offers I received from other firms came two to three months after my initial interview. I'll be long out of money by then.

My brain hurts, so I get out of the car and make my way to

the playground. I almost sit down on the battered old merry-go-round and then remember that I'm an adult in a white skirt suit. I don't need to add a rust stain to my troubles.

How easy were things back in elementary school? Back before I decided I couldn't tolerate living in Guntersville. Before boys were interesting, and most importantly before I could hear the voices. The voices of the dead.

I'm afraid I'm one more event away from cracking. A person can only take so many traumatic events before they are irreparably damaged. Sure, I'm resilient, at least that's what I believe, and people in my life have told me as much, but I know I'm fragile right now.

Sweat trickles down my spine. The tall oak trees surrounding the playground hold the ultraviolet rays from the sun off me. Still, they can't do anything to squelch the unbearable heat.

How pleasant would it be to transport back in time to elementary school? When my most significant concerns were whether Mama would let me spend the weekend with my cousin Tricia, or what was for dinner and if we'd have dessert.

I'm not doing too well with this adult stuff.

Screw the skirt suit. I don't care any longer if I ruin it, and I sit down on a swing. The cleaners can fix any damage I do. It's more important I revive my can-do attitude for what I must do now that my career has died a premature death.

Clutching the rusted chains tightly, I lean back and lift my legs. The canvas seat swings forward a few inches. I tuck my legs and gain momentum on the backward returning swing. Altitude comes quickly as I lean back with my legs plank straight in front of me, gliding through the moist, super-heated air.

Sometimes I need a change of scenery to change my perspective. It's not a walk on the beach or a boat ride on the lake, but feeling the breeze lift my long hair off my back as I swing forward takes a bit of the sting out of this morning.

Pushing and pulling harder, I gain enough momentum to be parallel with the ground at the top of my forward arc. I have the urge to jump off and fly—but don't.

It reminds me of the old trampoline and swing set my brothers and I had when we were kids. Chase, the more athletic of my two brothers, bet Dusty he could jump off the swing and land on the trampoline. As I remember, the distance was over twenty feet.

I was of the same mindset as Dusty; it couldn't be done. It seemed like at least twice as far as someone would be able to leap from the swing if they cleared it at all, and Chase has a long history of thinking he can pull a stunt off that he can't. Usually with catastrophic results.

Dusty continued to egg Chase on as he worked the swing to its maximum arc. I remember begging Chase not to try it, and all the while, he was giggling and talking trash to Dusty about how he was going to love spending Dusty's ten-dollar bill they bet.

The sensation of my heart stopping as I saw Chase leave the swing is still with me today. It appeared to be in slow motion. I watched my brother dismount gracefully from the swing and, at the last minute, twist his body, landing on his feet squarely on the trampoline. He put an exclamation on the stunt by going into a backflip. Which he also completed perfectly with his feet slightly apart. He immediately pointed at Dusty and yelled, "Pay up, sucker."

To this day, Chase's stunt is one of the coolest things I have ever seen. What wasn't cool was ten minutes later when Chase tried it again and slammed into the cast-iron side of the Olympic trampoline.

That earned us a trip to the emergency room. Mama was hollering at Dusty and me on the way to the hospital, demanding to know why we let him do it.

I'm sure it was rhetorical. Mama, if anyone, knows when Chase puts his mind to something, you can give up trying to talk him out of it.

Come to think of it, that describes everybody in my family—even me.

Okay, so now I have slammed into the side of my proverbial cast-iron trampoline. *What are you gonna do about it now, April?*

And that's the sixty-four-thousand-dollar question. The part that really bites is this isn't something I can Google or look up on YouTube. There is no friend I can call to advise me of my options and assist in developing a course of action. This is going to have to be a unique, tailor-made April May Snow plan.

Make no mistake about it. I might want to buy a bottle of Jack Daniels and drown my troubles while feeling sorry for myself. Or even a half-gallon of Bluebell cookies and cream ice cream and eat myself into sugar oblivion. Still, unlike when I was in college and knew things intrinsically would work out. There is an actual probability my dreams and aspirations have just been dealt a death blow.

If my future is going to be saved, I'll be the one doing it. There will be no family or friends coming to the rescue. Man, self-accountability is not all it's cracked up to be.

I let the swing's momentum slow and wait until it stops entirely so I don't have to scuff my yellow heels. I loop my arms around the chain and lean forward. My hair dangles in front of me.

Okay, don't get overwhelmed. Sure, it's a lot to take in all at once. Especially when I anticipated a pleasant leisurely orientation today and the firm buying my lunch at a nice restaurant.

But I don't want to be the girl who can't roll with the punches. I have always been able to take it as it comes, and as Granny Snow often says, "Make lemonade out of lemons."

First things first, I can't just ballpark my budget anymore. I need to get home and create a spreadsheet on my laptop and allocate every penny I own. That'll take care of the expense portion of the equation. Once I have that, it'll be easy to precisely determine how much time I have to find a new job and wait for the first paycheck.

The second half of the equation, and truthfully the part I dread, I must identify all the firms in Atlanta and contact them. I'll need to ask if they're taking applications. No, it doesn't sound like a lot of fun, and neither does going on scores of interviews over the next few weeks, but this is my future at risk.

If I can find a job in my profession that'll at least pay my rent and utilities, I'll take it. Even if I must wait tables on the weekend, at least I could stay in Atlanta and work in my profession. I'm not above working my way through an organization. I can delay buying a new car, and if I'm working on the weekends, I won't be able to spend money partying.

I just need a shot. Surely someone in this town will take a chance on me.

Chapter 5

I went straight to voice mail with the last two firms I called, where I was instructed their hours are eight to five Monday through Friday. I check the time and am shocked it is already after five.

When I ran my expenses on the ultra-cool Excel spreadsheet I created for my budget, I was horrified that I indeed have only six weeks' worth of expense money. That's with eating a lot of PB&Js and ramen noodles, four weeks if I eat normally, including fast food fixes.

The glaring issue on the expense sheet is the huge rent payment coming up in thirty days, which takes over half of my available funds. If it were not for the rent, I could have three months to find suitable employment and still have a little money to wait for the first payday.

Being hired in four weeks seems like a pipe dream, but that is the thread of hope I cling to.

One positive about an unrealistic goal, it makes you work with an incredible sense of urgency. I managed to call thirty-one firms in four hours, not counting the two that just went to voice mail.

I'm pumped about my insane level of commitment. I'm killing it on contacting all the firms in Atlanta about employment opportunities.

Unfortunately, I have only located two taking applications so far, and both said they would be interviewing for fall positions. I'll be homeless by the fall.

But I don't have to worry about that. Online, there are over two hundred and forty law firms in Atlanta alone. Over the next few days, I should be able to contact every one of them. There must be at least one firm looking for a bright young attorney to join their firm. It's just a numbers game.

I lean back in my kitchen chair and rub my eyes. It's either a numbers game or a war of attrition. I know I can't stop, but I'm also very aware that all I'm doing is blocking out my emotions because I don't have time to deal with them right now.

Someday, once I have a job in my profession, I'll take the time and mourn what should have been: the position I earned at the premier law firm in Atlanta. Then once I have dealt with the unfairness of what was rightfully mine being ripped out of my hands, I'll be even better prepared to scratch my way to the top of a different firm.

Who knows, maybe things *are* happening for a reason. There is the chance that what I'm supposed to do is eventually open my own firm and strike out, blazing a trail for a fresh style of legal services. It's not beyond comprehension to think I would have been stifled working in a firm that already had its own paradigms and client base.

That's what it is. I'm supposed to sharpen my skills at a small firm and then launch my own company. A practice I'll build into a mega-firm from the ground up. A firm with the prior reputation of MLJ, only earned ethically. That'll be something I can be proud of.

My phone rings, startling me from my mountain of glory. The number is Atlanta, and my heart leaps, knowing someone has come to their senses and called me back for an interview. "April May Snow," I say as I answer my phone.

"Well, now I know your real name."

The male voice on the phone sends electrical charges across my chest. "Who is this?"

"Hey, Bama. This is Shane. I just want to check in on you and make sure you're okay."

"Shane?"

"We met today at the law firm. You were looking for the human resources department."

I know who he is. I'm just surprised I'm talking to him right now. "Oh yeah, sure. What can I do for you?"

"Well, like I said, I just felt like I needed to check in on you. It seemed like you were having a pretty rotten day when you left the firm."

That's an understatement. "Yes, I have had better."

"I'm glad to know you made it home okay. That's a relief."

So odd. Shane's talking to me like he's known me all my life, and we had five minutes' worth of conversation between us, tops. "Yep. No troubles."

"Good. So how are you doing?"

I don't have time for this. For the second time today, I need to figure out the easiest way to end a conversation without being rude to Shane. "Great."

"Good. Did you have a backup plan you can bounce to since MLJ closed?"

The word "plan" tweaks two things in my mind simultaneously. First, Shane is someone who understands the importance of plans. This changes my perception of the big beautiful lug I met this morning.

The second thing the word "plan" does is aggravate me because I should have had a contingency plan. I'm still angry that I let MLJ string me along for the last two months and never once considered working on a backup in case my employment fell through. How naïve can I be?

I surprise myself and tell Shane the truth. "I should have, but I felt confident it was a done deal. I'm feeling pretty stupid about it right now."

"You shouldn't beat yourself up about that. Why would you have had any reason to expect the FBI to be raiding them this morning? Besides, it is what it is. Just swim with the current, and you'll get to where you want to go."

My first impression of Shane was definitely wrong. "I know you're right, but I have sort of painted myself into a corner now."

"Finances tight?"

I sigh. "Yep."

"That's rough. But we've all been there. You seem like the type who'll figure it out."

I wish I had the same level of confidence in my abilities. "I hope so. Otherwise, I'm going to have to move back home to my parents' house."

"At least you have a fallback position."

I snort a laugh. "Right, if I want to give up all my freedoms and put my career a decade behind schedule."

The line is quiet, and I wonder if I dropped Shane from the cell. "I doubt it can be that bad. You seem like you came from a good family to me."

The sarcasm of my statement seems overly harsh now, and my cheeks flush hot. "I just really want to make this happen in Atlanta."

"Then you will."

I laugh again. This stranger is a piece of work. "Just that simple?"

"No. But where hard work and desire intersect, you'll usually find success."

"Is there any chance your family is from Sand Mountain? Because you sound just like everyone in my family."

"No. Born and raised here in Fulton County. But I think truths are universal regardless of where you live."

I settle back in my chair and cross one arm over my chest as I hold the phone to my ear. "I suppose you're right. So now that you know my name, how about you reciprocate?"

"I thought you'd never ask. My last name is White."

"Well, thank you for the call, Shane White. You were right earlier. I did need someone to talk to, and I appreciate you filling the void."

"Glad to be of service."

"I better get back to drawing out my new plan for taking over Atlanta's legal market."

"Hey, before you go, have you had dinner yet? I'd love to continue the conversation."

My intent is to get Shane off the phone so I can continue to map out tomorrow's job hunt. Unless he is a lawyer or has family members who work for a firm, having dinner with him serves no purpose. I don't have time for the distraction.

Then why am I having such a difficult time telling him no?

I swallow hard and force myself to say, "I appreciate the offer, but I'm too busy right now."

"Oh, okay. I understand. But look, save my number. If you think of anything I can do to help you, please don't hesitate to give me a call."

"Sure, I appreciate that."

"Cool. Well, you have a good night, April Snow."

"You too, Shane White."

I stare at the phone for a few seconds after we disconnect the line. That may have been one of the most unusual phone calls I have ever had. Inexplicably, the fact Shane now calls me April instead of Bama makes me a little sad.

Chapter 6

Falling into my car, I fight back the tears of frustration I want to cry. My air conditioning has been struggling against the brutal Atlanta heat the last few days, which adds to my exasperation. The last thing I need now is for the air conditioning in my car to give out.

I stare at the oak door of the small brick office that houses Lewis and Mays, the three-person law firm that just interviewed me. Honestly, two months ago, I wouldn't have even considered interviewing at a firm like Lewis and Mays. It's two partners and a legal assistant who doubles as the receptionist in a rundown area of Marietta, Georgia. It is also my last opportunity for employment this week.

This Friday evening, I should have been celebrating the completion of my first week at MLJ at a ritzy bar in downtown Atlanta. Instead, I'm contemplating if dinner will be two packs of ramen noodles or if I want to splurge and pick a couple items off the dollar value meal on the way home.

Instead of sitting on a barstool, enjoying a margarita or blackberry sangria, I'm sitting in my car. My panties feel like they've welded to my butt due to my sweat.

That's only the beginning of my issues.

If my limited budget and the weak job market aren't enough, this week's interviews convinced me it would be impossible to find employment until I passed the bar exam.

It seems other firms are not as impressed with my having graduated at the top of my class at Alabama. In some ways, it's even a detriment. They believe as soon as I get a better opportunity, I'll leave them.

In fact, that's a fair assessment, although I'd rather them ignore that inconvenient truth. Besides, my short tenure at their firm still must be better for them than hiring someone without my talent. Either way, not already having my license to practice is a severe impediment to my employment in Atlanta.

On the positive, MLJ had enrolled me for the next sitting of the bar exam and paid for the testing fee. On the negative, the exam is still five weeks away, and it'll be another month after the test before I receive the results.

That's assuming I pass the bar on my first sitting. Not always a given and looking less and less likely since I have not begun studying for it. How can I? I'm spending every waking hour calling for interviews that provide a minimal opportunity for me to land a position.

I'm stuck in a genuine conundrum. I can't land a position because I have not passed the bar exam. I won't be able to pass the bar if I don't create the time to study. But I'll be out of money way before I get confirmation I'm licensed and get employment.

The math isn't working in my favor. I have enough cash for another five weeks in Atlanta, but I'm looking at a nine-week timeline. Nine weeks to pass the bar, gain employment, and receive my first paycheck.

All this is making my head hurt. I start my car and join the long procession of traffic heading in the direction of my apartment.

My hands begin to shake, and I grip the steering wheel tighter. I can feel myself sliding closer and closer to the edge. The abyss that will take me to a dark place I don't have time for right now.

But it's all there. The numbers don't lie. It may already be game over for my life dreams, and I'm too hard-headed to accept it.

Maybe I should just call Mama and tell her I'm coming home.

The release of the pressure off me would be welcome. At least I wouldn't feel like my head is about to explode, or my heart will beat out of my chest.

Twenty-seven is awfully young to have a heart attack or a stroke. Still, this stressful situation seems pretty intent on putting me in an early grave.

Lord knows it would be the right decision. Deep down, I know my family would be disappointed *for* me but not disappointed *in* me. They would understand, and they would help me regroup and try again under better circumstances.

It's not like it was my fault anyway. How was I supposed to know MLJ was under investigation? It's not exactly something a law student can Google and find out about a prospective employer. It's not like you're going to find something that says, "The three principal partners of MLJ are highly suspected of money laundering."

I'm still ticked off that my psychic abilities didn't give me a heads up. I'd been in the building and not felt the first thing sketchy about the firm. If anything, everything felt exciting and new. I remember the adrenaline rush I felt during my interviews with all the partners this past spring.

That's stupid. I was so pumped about the opportunity and proud of it, Beelzebub could've asked me to sign a contract in blood, and I wouldn't have had a moment's hesitation. As Mama used to say, "Foolish, foolish girl."

I have certainly put myself in a bind this time. Atlanta isn't going to be merciful and allow me to pull myself out of it. That's one thing I can say about a small town. When you're down, if people can, they'll give you a hand up. The big-city mentality is best summed up by Jan Miller on the day my life ended. "Sucks for you."

I only see one last opportunity to buy myself enough time to take the bar exam and get a job. I must extend my money further. Even if I don't eat for the next nine weeks, my money will be long gone before hearing about my score.

Since day one, I've been considering it, but I just have not had the heart to talk to the leasing agent about my contract. It kills me to think getting rid of the apartment I was so excited about scoring is the only option left. If I can get out from under the lease payment that'll be due next month, I can stretch out my money long enough and stay in the game.

I'm not sure where I'll sleep during that time. Still, I suppose if I have to sleep in my car for a few weeks at a rest stop, it's a small price to pay. I'm not worried about a shower. I can join a fitness gym for ten dollars a month and take my showers there.

The thought of self-imposed homelessness, on the one hand, seems crazy. But I really want to make this happen, and it looks like one of the few options left to me to allow my dreams to happen. It's just temporary, and I can do anything temporarily.

I'm torn between if it makes more sense to sell my furniture for the extra cash I might be able to make on a quick sale or if it is smarter to store it. But storage will cost money, plus I'd have to rent a truck. I also don't know if I can lift all of it by myself. It'll be best to sell it for what I can get.

It's just stuff anyway. Once I land my dream job, I'll buy new and better stuff.

Chapter 7

I pull into my apartment parking lot and trudge to the leasing agent's office. My stomach is churning, and I feel sick.

One break. I just need one good break, and everything good will come my way.

Putting on a fake wide smile, I open the door and step into the office. It is blessedly cool inside the small room.

The desk where the leasing agent sat when I signed my lease papers is empty. I hear voices through an open door to the right. "Hello?"

The voices stop, and a man pokes his head in from the doorway. "Oh, hi. I didn't hear you come in."

The tall, attractive man with copper-colored skin is not the agent who leased the apartment to me. To make nice, I step forward and extend my hand. "I'm April Snow. I'm renting 303L."

"Glad to have you. Are you going to the hospitality party tonight at the pool? We'd love to see you there."

I wring my hands. "No. Actually, I need to un-lease my apartment."

"Excuse me?" He tilts his head and squints.

"Un-lease my apartment? I can't afford it."

"Honey, there are a lot of folks here who can't afford the rent," he says.

"Right, but I don't have a job, and I won't be able to pay for my upcoming rent."

He nods his head. "And your point?"

"I need to get out of my lease before we run into that situation."

"Right, it doesn't work that way. You are on the hook for whatever the lease length you signed unless your company relocated you. Is that what happened?"

The urge to lie is considerable, but I just can't. "No, the company I work for closed unexpectedly."

"I'm sorry. Was it, April?"

I nod my head.

"That's a bad break. Believe me, I wish I could help you out, but the lease has very few options to break it. Actually, there is only one. If you're relocated. I don't know what your situation is. Unfortunately, you're on the hook for the rent regardless of whether your company is closed."

"But I'm here to tell you I can't pay for it. Isn't there something we can work out?"

His face twists into a frown as he looks down at the ground. "I wish there were. Basically, the rental company doesn't care whether you make the payment or not. If you don't, they'll just take you to court for the full amount plus penalty charges and court costs. I have seen it before, and they get their money regardless."

"That's ridiculous." I rest my hands on my hips as I scowl at him.

"I don't make the rules. I just process the paperwork for the company."

"April?"

I look toward the backroom door where the familiar voice comes from. I blink hard as I recognize Shane standing in the doorway.

"I thought I heard your voice," he says with a smile as he approaches me. "What are you doing here?"

"I guess wasting my time." I point toward the leasing agent.

"Carl," he says.

"Carl's time, too."

Shane looks from Carl to me and back to Carl. "I don't understand."

"She's lost her job, and she's trying to get out of her lease," Carl says.

Shane points at me. "She's the girl I was telling you about. The one that walked in at MLJ the day they closed them down."

"Seriously?" Carl's eyebrows lift. "Okay, I understand you better now, Shane."

It's disconcerting that Shane was talking to someone about me. I'm about to ask what Carl understands better now when Shane interjects, "So you live here, too?"

"At the moment. But I can't afford it." I'm wondering how a furniture mover can afford an apartment complex like this one. But then again, if he's friends with Carl, he might also pull shifts as a leasing agent and get a significant discount if not free rent.

"I have been here for about three years now. It's a fun place to live." He frowns and scratches his head. "That was stupid of me to say, given the situation you're in. I didn't mean to be insensitive."

"We're good. I guess we'll be neighbors until they throw me out on the street since we can't work it out."

"Dang, Carl. You're really gonna be all harsh and hang a huge bill around this girl's neck?"

"Man, don't even."

Shane shrugs. "Just doesn't seem like the deal you cut with Manny when he left. Come to think of it, I think Katie got a pretty sweet deal, too."

"You're the worst friend ever, Shane."

He laughs. "Probably."

I'm more than ready to leave. I don't understand the discussion going on between the two men. Quite frankly, I need to crawl back to my temporary home and lick my wounds. Before they throw me out on my keister and hand me a twenty-thousand-dollar invoice for nothing.

"All right, April. This is how it works," Carl says to me. "Get me something that says your company has closed. At the same time, I need a letter from a company more than ninety miles away saying they've employed you. If you can get me those two things, I can get you out of the lease. Understand you'll be able to stay until the end of the month, but you lose your deposit."

The idea of losing the eighteen-hundred-dollar deposit doesn't sit well with me. Still, it certainly beats having a twenty-thousand-dollar expense tied to the top of my student loans that are about to start needing to be paid. "Thank you."

Carl nods. "Understand it has to be as legit as possible. I need this job."

"I understand. I wouldn't put you in jeopardy for helping me."

"Good. You must get it to me by the end of the day Monday. I need to get this paperwork in as soon as possible."

"Okay." I turn to Shane. "And thank you for your help."

He flashes his uber-sexy smile. "Don't mention it. I love any opportunity I get to make Carl uncomfortable."

Carl shakes his head. "I don't know why I keep you for a friend."

"Because I'm the only one who'll put up with your whining." Shane turns his attention back to me. "You owe me dinner."

He catches me by surprise, and the pressure has built up so high in my body, I bark a laugh. Embarrassingly unladylike. "I do?"

Both guys laugh at me. Shane sobers first. "Yes, you do."

"I hope you like Dinty Moore stew or Armour chili. Those are the two fanciest things I've got left in my cupboard."

"No and no. Besides, I'm not gonna steal food from a working girl who's down on her luck. I was offering to buy."

Little red alarms start screeching and flashing in my mind. Understand, I'm extremely attracted to Shane. And under any other circumstances, I would love to go out on a date with him. But already, I feel myself becoming increasingly indebted to him. I don't like the idea of being beholden to anyone because of their charity or goodwill. Call me a cynic, but the tab always comes due.

It would be a totally different dynamic if I could buy Shane's dinner. If I were not short on cash, I'd offer to buy both men dinner tonight since they had saved me a considerable amount of money by doing me a solid. But I'm not in that position.

"No strings attached," Shane says as he seems to read my mind. "I just have to go to work in a couple of hours, so I can't go home and eat dinner with my family. Carl has already turned me down, and I'd rather not eat alone. Look at it as if you're doing me a favor."

I know I'm not actually doing him a favor, and he's just trying to make it easier on me. But the fact is, I'd like to learn more about him. Learn more than the fact his voice makes the skin tingle across my chest, and his smile causes my knees to turn weak. "Okay. As long as it's nothing fancy and it's not a date."

"Do you like catfish?"

I roll my eyes at him. "Do you come on this strong with all the girls?"

"You do?" He raises his eyebrows.

"Yes. Careful, or you'll win my heart, and you won't be able to get rid of me."

"There could be worse things to happen to a guy," he says.

Chapter 8

Pausing, I lean back as heat flushes my face. I'm self-conscious I have dominated the conversation during dinner. I told Shane about my difficulties finding employment and the challenge of studying for the bar exam while figuring out my impossible finances. Through it all, he's nodded agreement and listened.

Unlike my brothers, he hasn't offered a single idea on how to fix the issues. He seems content to watch me scarf down a massive amount of fried catfish, white beans, turnip greens, and hush puppies.

"Tell me, Shane. Do you work with Carl? I mean, are you one of the leasing agents, too?"

Shane shakes his head and grins. "Nah. I just like to check in on Carl from time to time. He really is a good guy. He just doesn't do conflict very well."

"He shut me down pretty quick. If it were not for you, he wouldn't have lifted a finger to help me."

"He was just intimidated by you. It's a lot easier to hide behind the rules if someone intimidates you."

I point to my chest. "I'm intimidating?"

"Yes."

"He's a good six inches taller than me and at least eighty pounds heavier. How can I be intimidating?"

Shane laughs as he leans back and tosses his napkin on the

table. "Have you ever looked in the mirror when you're upset?"

"Have I what? No, why would I?"

He rolls a shoulder. "It might open your eyes to why people react a certain way toward you."

"Well, that's rather rude."

"I don't mean it to be. But it is the truth."

"Whatever."

We both turn silent. I pick at the coleslaw left on my plate. I'll eat coleslaw, but it's not one of my favorites.

"If I'm so intimidating, why did you ask me out to dinner?"

"I guess I find you interesting. Plus, I don't scare as easily as most men."

That gets my attention, and when I look up, our eyes lock. Shane laughs, and I join him. "You're incorrigible."

"I resemble that remark," he says.

"You mentioned you didn't have time to go home tonight to eat with your family. Do you live with your parents?"

"No. They live up in Virginia."

I feel like I must pump Shane for every bit of information. It's exhausting. "So, who were you planning on eating dinner with if you had the time to get home?"

"My Pop. He lives alone. I try to eat dinner with him whenever possible."

I wasn't expecting that, and my eyes well with tears at the thought. I'm not sure if it's because I'm missing my grand-mothers who both live by themselves or if it's the guilt factor that I should but rarely do take the time to visit and eat a meal with them.

Who is this boy? I don't know if I have ever met anyone so in-trinsically nice and thoughtful in my entire life.

"That's sweet of you."

"Not really. I enjoy his company." He points at me. "I enjoy your company, too."

I scoff. "Right. I'm such great company because I talk all the way through dinner and don't give you a chance to say any-thing."

"I would have said something if I wanted to."

I stare him in the eye and realize I trust him and I'd appreciate his opinion. I have been attempting to develop an effective plan for four days, and I could use his objective input. "What do you think? About my situation?"

Shane leans forward, resting his elbows on the table as he places his hands together and rests his chin. He looks up and says, "I think you're majorly screwed."

The words are like a slap across my face, and my jaw drops.

"I'm just playing." He laughs.

"That's just wrong."

"I know. I couldn't resist."

"Well, thanks for dinner." I set my napkin on my plate and begin to stand. He reaches across the table and lays his hand on mine. I feel the golden warmth of his spirit.

"Come on now, I was just teasing."

"That was mean."

"Yes, but I wanted to get your attention before I tell you this."

I settle back in my chair and give Shane my best "this better be good" stare.

"You're only attacking this on the expense side. There are two parts to this equation. You should work on the other side, too. Make more income."

I raise my hands. "Did you hear me? I have been all over town. I can't find a position."

"An attorney's position. And you even said that technically in a lot of the folks' eyes, you aren't even an attorney yet because you haven't passed the bar."

"Thanks for reminding me."

Shane sighs heavily. "Dang, girl. Can you slow down with the defensiveness?"

If I was defensive, it's because I feel like I'm being judged by Shane. His reiterating the weakness on my résumé isn't exactly helpful to me.

"What I'm trying to say is, if you were to take another job, not necessarily in the legal profession, but a job that could bring in some income, you could extend the length of time you're able to stay in Atlanta. The longer you can stay here, the more probable you'll pass the bar exam and find employment at a firm."

"Except if I'm working some crap job to make grocery money, I won't have any time to study."

"That's not true. It just depends on the job. There are some jobs where you can study a good bit of the time you're there."

I hear Shane, and I'm trying to think of a single job where I can study while earning some cash. Absolutely nothing comes to mind. "That sounds great. Where do I sign up for this mystery job?"

Shane either doesn't understand my heavy tone of sarcasm, or he chooses to ignore it. "Perfect. Let me check with my friend tonight. Do you think you're available in the morning?"

I squinch my face. "For what?"

"I'm sure she'll want to interview you, but I know she'll love you." He points at me. "Well, not that suspicious expression so much, but your normal face."

"You're serious?"

He nods. "Yeah. Dr. Hamlin has a position open. It is typically filled by students who spend a lot of time studying when they're not needed. But it's working with patients at the hospital. You're not queasy about blood or other body fluids, are you?"

"No."

"Great. I'll talk to her about it tonight."

I can't keep the frown off my face as I ask, "Shane, why are you doing all this?"

"You seem like you could use some help, and I can." He flashes a sexy grin at me. "You'd do the same thing if the roles were reversed."

I'd like to think that, but I'm not positive. Shane has a much higher opinion of me than I do.

Chapter 9

As I slip into an old T-shirt and brush my teeth, getting ready for bed, I can't get Shane out of my head. He's certainly one of the oddest people I have ever met.

Granny would call him an old spirit. How Shane carries himself and speaks is more like someone who's lived many more years than he has.

It's difficult to believe there is a position where I'll be able to study and earn an income. Cash that'll extend the time I have before I'm forced to call it quits, tuck my tail, and run home to Guntersville.

Even though I have known him for an extremely brief time, I trust Shane. If he says there is such a position, if he thinks he can help me get the job, well, I must believe him.

I run a brush through my hair. The humidity has curled it so badly it doesn't want to let go of all the knots. I finally give up and put the brush down. I'll fight that battle in the morning.

Exhausted, but with a full stomach and hopeful things might still work out, I slide into bed. As I reach over to turn out the light, my cell phone rings.

I groan when I see that it's Mama. I'd be lying if I said I don't consider ignoring the call. But I know she'll just call back.

"Hey, Mama."

"Is this my missing daughter?"

I roll my eyes. "I'm sorry I have not called, Mama."

"Oh, no worries here. We all know you're busy with your new law firm. It's okay if your mama and daddy end up in the hospital with anxiety issues because we have not heard from you in five days."

"No news is good news?" I offer tentatively.

"Hmm, our only daughter living by herself in a strange large city. No, I think we'd rather hear from you at least once a day, even if it's just a text."

I don't want to admit it, but I know she has a point. "I'm sorry. I'll do better."

"Well, tell me how it is. Dusty said you have a very swanky young professional apartment."

For a few more days, at least. "Yes, ma'am. It's really nice."

"And the job? How's that going?"

"It's challenging." I grit my teeth after telling the white lie and am thankful she's not talking to me face to face.

"You always did enjoy a challenge. I'm sure you'll do fine."

"Yes, ma'am."

"I'm glad to hear you're doing well. The main reason why I called is I want to know if you will be up for the weekend. The boys and your daddy are planning on grilling ribs, and we have not seen you in a while. We would love to catch up with you."

"Gee, I can't this weekend."

"No?"

"No, I'm afraid I have already got too much work to do. It's a real pain just trying to get fully acclimated to working full time again." Since I got away with the first little lie, I'm confident in my ability to weave more detailed stories.

"I'm sure everyone will be disappointed."

"Me too. I hate to miss out on ribs this weekend," I say.

"No worries, I'll UPS you a slab Monday."

Ouch. Harsh. Mama can play hardball with the best of them. I laugh to play it off as a joke. "I think I'll pass on that."

She sighs heavily. "Well, if you're ever able to carve out a little time for your family, please let us know so we'll make sure to be home."

Where else would they be? Dusty didn't mention our parents had started traveling. "I will."

"Sleep tight, career girl. Don't forget to text me occasionally and let me know you're all right."

"I will. Good night, Mama."

I hang up and turn out the light. Despite the fact I'm exhausted, I can't fall asleep now. I wonder how long I can keep up the charade with my parents. I don't like deceiving them, but I also don't want to have a conversation about what went wrong, and they ask me what my plans are when I'm not sure.

It's not totally improbable that I might be able to land a position in the next few weeks, and they'll never know the difference. I could always tell them I received a better offer and left MLJ. I know it will be a tough sell, considering how much I talked up MLJ's practice, but since none of them are attorneys, they will never be the wiser.

That's not true. My uncle, Howard, will know, and he would be sure to tell them what caliber of a firm I'm working for. Having an attorney for an uncle is becoming very inconvenient.

Thanks, Mama. I was feeling better about myself until you called. Now I'm ashamed of lying and feeling moderately depressed.

Chapter 10

It's noon on Friday, and I'm about to call it a day. I have been grinding for the last three days and only scheduled a handful of longshot opportunities. I'm not sure if it's because it's Friday or if my voice sounds despondent, but today is the worst. A complete strikeout. Nobody wants to talk about any current positions or positions in the future. This is one of those days when I should have stayed in bed feeling sorry for myself.

My phone rings. It's an Atlanta area code, and even though I have not saved his number, I recognize it as Shane's. "Hello."

"What are you doing right now?"

"Striking out on the job front."

"Not anymore. Are you dressed?"

"Yeah." I drag out my answer for five syllables.

"I talked to Janet, and she wants to meet you."

"The doctor with the job?"

"Right. I'm sending you the address, office number, and her cell number. I need you to get there in the hour. She's leaving early for an extended weekend, and she won't be back until Tuesday."

"What should I wear?"

"Nothing too fancy. But no shorts."

Not helpful. "Do I need a résumé?"

"No, I have already convinced her she needs to hire you. She just wants to meet you first." There is a commotion, and Shane is talking to someone else.

"Shane?"

"Hey, April, I gotta go. You won't need it, but good luck."

He cuts me off. I stare at my phone in disbelief. A text comes across with all the information Shane promised. He helpfully noted that the drive takes twenty minutes from the apartment.

Awesome. That means I have about fifteen minutes to get ready, considering I don't know where I'll be parking. It's a good thing I at least took a shower this morning. Maybe it was best I got out of bed after all.

Yes, there is a part of me that feels dirty about all this. I am lying to my family and relying on complete strangers for help.

I pick a khaki skirt and a plain white blouse. Then I pull my hair back in a low ponytail. Professional, but ready to work. Or at least that's what I'm hoping it implies. I have no idea how to dress for a medical position.

I grab my purse and keys and head out to my car. I pause as I unlock the car door.

What in the world are you doing, April? Just go home, study for the bar exam, and once you pass it, you can look for a job in Hunts-ville or Birmingham like most of the other Alabama grads are doing.

That is the most logical plan. I'd have plenty of peace and quiet at my parents' to study. I wouldn't have to worry about my finances over the next two months. At the end of the summer, I'd leave Guntersville again to start fresh, but this time with my full credentials.

I wrench open the door to my car and fall into the blistering-hot bucket seat.

Going home makes all the sense in the world. But this is the one time in my life I choose not to be sensible. I'm aware I have been dealt an incredibly crappy hand, but I'm holding out hope that when the river turns, I'll still come up a winner.

Besides, no matter how much salt you put on it, crow always tastes terrible.

The traffic is thankfully light due to everyone going in the opposite direction. As I circle the parking deck searching for a spot, I notice my hands are sweating profusely.

I'm surprised I'm nervous about interviewing for a temporary position. But a temporary job has never held so much sway over my future.

A slot comes open for me on the third floor. I take the elevator to the basement where Dr. Hamlin's office is located.

The elevator doors open, and I get a chill. That makes sense. The basement feels at least ten degrees cooler than the third floor because we're underground. That would keep the basement naturally cooler than the upper floors.

Walking to Dr. Hamlin's office, I stop and have an anxiety party. I never asked Shane what I'd be doing at this job. I can't remember ever interviewing for a position and not knowing something about the work duties and the company. I have never been this unprepared in my life, and it gives me the sensation of being naked.

It's too late to worry about my lack of preparation now. I'll just have to ad-lib to the best of my ability and act like Shane has thoroughly explained the job duties to me.

I should be close now, but I begin to feel a little off. I can't put my finger on it, but I sense a doozy of a headache coming on, and my stomach is all bubbly. I guess my nerves are doing a number on me.

Dr. Hamlin's office door is open. I knock on the doorjamb before stepping in. There is an empty desk in front of me.

I check my phone as I become concerned I missed her. Shane did say she was leaving for an early weekend.

"Hello?" I hear a high-pitched female voice.

I notice a door behind the desk slightly ajar. The voice came from the room behind the door.

"Hi, I'm looking for Dr. Hamlin."

The door opens, and a woman well over six feet tall and weighing in at three hundred pounds if she's an ounce appears. "You must be Shane's April."

"Uh, yes, ma'am. April Snow." She threw me for a loop the way she said Shane's.

"Shane sure does think highly of you. He says you're as smart as they come."

"I hope he didn't oversell me."

She pushes her lower lip out. "Impossible. Shane is an incredible judge of character. What he's not good at is communicating details to people. I hope he has the right of things as I have my reservations now that I see you. But I don't take to people who judge a book by its cover, so I'll have to extend the same courtesy."

I have no idea what Janet is referring to. I can feel the stupid smile on my face, and I wish I could change it.

"I bet he didn't tell you anything about this job."

The room feels abnormally hot. "He told me a little bit about it."

She raises her eyebrows. "What did he say you'd be doing?"

As I stare at her, I realize my mouth is open. I thought I would be able to wing this interview, but Janet hasn't given me any details to construct an impromptu outline of duties to regurgitate to her.

"He didn't tell you a darn thing, did he?"

"No, ma'am."

She laughs. "That boy is good as gold, but he tends to omit things he believes might be a deal-breaker. I suppose he snookered both of us."

I'm glad Janet finds our situation humorous, but I'm starting to become concerned. Plus, my headache is threatening to turn into a migraine.

"Do you have your social security card and your driver's license?"

"Yes, ma'am."

"I'm sorry if I'm in a rush. My partner is picking me up in a few minutes, and we're driving to the coast tonight. Just us girls until Tuesday." Her smile is proportionate to the rest of her.

"That sounds fun. What part?"

"Destin. Hopefully, it won't be too crowded."

"You can always hope," I say.

"I know. The last time we were down there, our umbrella was three back from the water. I have never seen so many saggy old butts in my entire life."

"That's an expensive vacation for that view."

Janet finishes scanning my documents. "You can say that again, sister."

She hands me my cards as a smallish young man with red hair standing on end comes into the office. He's dressed in rumpled blue scrubs. "Hey, Doc. Aren't you about to shove off?"

"You know it, Ricky. Be a dear and take April to the supply room and get her a pair of scrubs." Janet turns her attention to me. "The laundry service takes care of the cleaning for us, so just drop them off at the end of your shift. You can wear something more comfortable to work if you prefer. Jeans and a T-shirt are fine since you're going to change into the scrubs anyway."

"I don't understand," I say.

Janet squints her eyes. "Don't understand what, honey?"

I turn my hands over and shrug. "What are we doing?"

"Well, I'm going to the beach. And you two are working the second shift tonight. Then, April, you've got the seven a.m. to seven p.m. shift Saturday and Sunday."

My head is swimming as I'm trying to understand what's going on. I don't even know what I'm doing yet, and I'm panicking. The migraine radiates across my skull, and I wince. It feels like an ice pick was inserted at the back of my neck. "I got the job?"

"Yes, you did." Janet squeezes between Ricky and me. "Ricky, show her the ropes. I'll see you Wednesday."

"Will do. Don't do anything I wouldn't, Doc."

She stops, turns, and tilts her head. "Is there anything you wouldn't do, Ricky?"

"Come to think of it, probably not."

"That's what I thought. You two have fun."

As the two of them joke, I'm wondering what in the world I have done. I have no idea what I just signed up for, no idea what I'm being paid, and have already been assigned three shifts.

"She's a great boss to work for," Ricky says.

"She seems nice." That's all I can work up in my present state of confusion.

Ricky gestures for me to follow him. "Let's go get you those scrubs."

He locks the door behind us. As I wait for him, he adds, "There is a women's locker near the supply room. You can store your stuff in there if you bring a lock tomorrow. You'll probably want to keep them in the office today, though."

There are so many questions bouncing around in my head; I don't even know where to start. But one thing's for sure: I have been thrown a lifeline regardless of what I'm doing, and I am grateful for it. Even at minimum wage, three shifts are a hundred and fifty dollars of grocery money I didn't have coming into me an hour ago.

That's the logical, practical, extraordinary-work-ethic April talking in my head. She's doing her best to scream down always-in-control April who likes to know every detail before committing to something. There is a real civil war going on in my mind.

"The best advice I can give you is to bring a book or have some good games on your phone. The most difficult part about this job is staying awake. Not that anyone would care if they caught you napping," Ricky says.

"How long have you been working for Dr. Hamlin?"

"About a year now. Eventually, I want to get back into school, but the timing hasn't been right."

"What do you mean?"

He cuts his blue eyes at me. "I suppose that's code for 'I'm not ready to buckle down and study yet.'"

"Ah, now that I understand."

Ricky unlocks a door with his security card. I follow him in, and we are in a small break room with a TV set to the news.

"You can come in here and take your breaks if you want to. But honestly, with nobody hardly ever in the office, there is really no point in coming down here." He reaches for a pile of scrubs, stops, and turns to examine me.

"What's the matter?" I ask.

"Nothing, you're just a mismatch."

"What does that mean?"

He pulls two tops out of one pile and two bottoms out of a second. "When you need more, get the small size pants and the medium size tops."

Ricky's just being helpful, but the idea he can size my clothes by looking at me is a bit awkward. It won't hurt my feelings if he's wrong when I try them on and I must change them out for a different size.

The exchange doesn't faze him as he walks further back into the break room and points to the left. "There is a locker room there for the ladies. How about you meet me back at the office when you're ready. That way, I won't be leaving the office unattended for too long."

"Sure, that'll work." Plus, it'll allow me to change up to the size I need without him knowing.

He lifts his chin. "Cool. I'll see you in a few."

The door clicks shut behind Ricky. I stand still and stare at the silver doorknob.

I could put the scrubs back on the shelf and leave right now. It would be incredibly immature of me, but I am completely overwhelmed with the speed this is happening. I don't know if I'll be expected to mop floors, escort family members to patient rooms, or change dirty sheets.

It doesn't really matter what they need me to do. Work is work. Every job I have ever done has some part about it that really bites. They all have that one really nice aspect of getting a check on payday, too. So, what's eating at me? Why does every impulse in my body implore me to run to my car?

It's probably just the idea of being in a hospital. I have been fortunate and never spent much time in one. The little bit of time Grandpa Snow spent in the hospital before he passed was enough to convince me there is not much good that can come of being at one. This is just a feeling I'll be afflicted with and have to control until I become numb to my surroundings. Hours of labor in a hospital will make me less sensitive to the environment.

That's what the issue is. It's like my skin is crawling. Little tingles are sparkling up and down my arms, and the threat of the next spike of my migraine is so much on my mind I feel like I may bring it sooner with a self-fulfilling prophecy.

No, this is good. It sounds like the job doesn't require a tremendous amount of effort. If Ricky is suggesting I need a book, then Shane is precisely correct. This could be my study session to prepare for the bar exam.

I'm still in disbelief. How is it possible to be fortunate enough to meet Shane? Someone who has put me in a position to be successful in Atlanta.

Me wanting to run earlier? That's because I don't feel like I deserve this opportunity. I'm not usually prone to self-sabotage, but I have been through a lot the past few months, and my self-esteem is tattered.

Why wouldn't my confidence be at an all-time low? I have had the trauma of being shot at, strangled, and even watching a woman burn alive. That's a lot of bad to unpack in just a few months.

My gosh, I'm most likely suffering from some sort of PTSD. I know I shouldn't try to self-diagnose myself, especially since I have no medical expertise. Still, surely all the events that happened recently are taking a toll on my psyche.

Then throw on top of it, my dream job was ripped from my hands in the first hour of employment. That would be enough to make anybody curl into a fetal position.

Plus, the issue I keep wanting to ignore that keeps coming to light—my paranormal abilities.

Wait a second, other than feeling the warmth of Shane's spirit, I have not had the first hint of psychic activity since I arrived in Atlanta. Oh my gosh, that's fabulous.

My suspicions were right. I knew once I came to Atlanta, just like when I moved to Tuscaloosa for college, my paranormal abilities would atrophy, go silent, and eventually disappear altogether.

Thank you, Lord. The constriction of my chest releases and my shoulders relax. I feel better already.

Lately, I have been concerned as the paranormal weirdness which has afflicted me from the age of twelve has ran rampant. I feared it would soon absorb my entire being.

I'm not exaggerating. It was to the point I was constantly experiencing paranormal events.

But now—now that I'm focused on my working future—just blissful normalcy.

Grinning, I lift the scrubs Ricky selected for me and walk into the women's changing room. A few days ago, I thought my dreams were finished. But today? Today I'm optimistic things happen for a reason. I'm exactly where I'm supposed to be.

To my chagrin, Ricky selected the perfect size scrubs for me. I'm able to get over the weirdness as I stretch in my new work attire. They're like a stiff version of pajamas. Too bad I didn't study to be a nurse or a doctor. This is much more comfortable than thin, tight skirts and high heels.

He's right. I'll want to pick up a lock and store my belongings in the ladies' room tomorrow and Sunday. As I carry my belongings back to the office, I enter *Pick up lock* in my phone under tasks.

Looking up from my phone, I see Ricky standing at the door of the office. I wonder if he thought I wouldn't be able to find my way back.

"Perfect timing. We actually have a customer on the way," he says.

"Great. Can you show me where to keep my stuff today?"

He gestures for me to follow him back into the office, and we pass by the desk and through the door to Dr. Hamlin's. "I'm sure Janet won't mind you keeping your stuff in her office today. Nobody should be coming back here."

My eyes scan Janet's personal space. She has a BS degree from Auburn and a medical degree from UAB. Her family photos feature her with an attractive middle-aged woman and a little boy at various ages, from a baby to a six-year-old.

A portion of her L-shaped desk is cleared off, and I lay my belongings there.

Ricky reacts to a text on the phone he's carrying. "They're here."

As I follow him out of the office, he explains, "I have already filled out the paperwork for this patient. We're sort of going at this backward where you'll see the release process first, and then I'll show you the paperwork that typically comes when we first get the call."

I have an uncontrollable number of butterflies threatening to overturn my stomach. "What exactly do we do?"

"Patient discharge. There is not much to it. Still, all the paperwork must be completed properly so there are never any questions later," Ricky says as we continue down the sloped hallway.

Talk about life looking up. Who would have thought there is a specialized position at the hospital just for releasing patients? This is an unbelievably sweet gig.

My spirits lighten as I think how great it'll be to wheel patients who have recovered from the hospital as their family greets them. I smile with giddy anticipation as I visualize helping new moms and their excited husbands out to the car. I can't wait to help them attach their baby's car seat securely into the car for the first time.

I'll have to watch some YouTube videos on how to best secure car seats so I can be helpful. I'll want to spend some time on the best ways to help patients get out of the wheelchair into a car, too.

My shoulders stretch back as my posture improves, and my steps feel lighter. I'm going to enjoy this. I enjoy helping people, and what better time to share in folks' lives than when they're jubilantly discharged from a hospital stay. Yes, I need the money, but this is a job I might have volunteered for if I had the time, just to give me a sense of helping and, in general, pick my spirits up.

It's weird the hospital pays somebody to be a discharge attendant. It seems like it might be something you'd have a volunteer do. Don't they have candy stripers anymore?

"How's it going, Big Walter?" Ricky says to a man standing by a broad set of double doors.

"Honestly, I'm struggling to keep my head above water. Business has been a little too good lately," the short, stocky middle-aged man says.

Ricky pulls out a set of keys and unlocks the double doors. As he does, I notice Walter has a hand on a gurney left in the hallway.

My germaphobia kicks in, and I recoil. I'd have to wash my hands fifty times if I accidentally touched an unattended gurney.

Walter's eyes meet mine, and his purple-colored lips pull back on his gray face. "I don't believe we've met." He extends his hand. "I'm Walter Finebaum."

I stare at his extended hand, the hand that has just left the gurney, and hesitate. Against my better judgment, I decide Walter is someone important if Ricky knows him by first name basis, and I cringe as I extend my hand. "Glad to meet you, Walter. I'm April Snow."

"April just hired on with us. She's working with me today, and then she'll be working the weekend shift."

Walter holds eye contact with me. "Well, congratulations. No offense, but I hope I won't see you this weekend. I'm already covered up."

I don't understand what all this business talk and too much work have to do with walking discharged patients to their cars. Rather than ask, I decide I'll figure it out before too long.

I'm still looking at the odd covering on the gurney when I hear the click of the double doors. The hinges squeak as Ricky pushes the door open. A psychic wave rolls over me, snapping my attention to the small room revealed inside.

Ricky and Walter step inside. Walter pulls the gurney behind him. I'm still trying to understand the purpose of the room. It's a ten-foot square with a shelf to the right and another large door to the left with a cloudy glass porthole.

A sharp pain stabs my lower neck and sends excruciating discomfort across my scalp, causing me to wince. I fight back the desire to hold my head. The last thing I need is for Ricky and Walter to think I'm some sort of wacko when I have not worked a full day yet.

Ricky and Walter sign some sort of book the size of an old-timey photo album on the shelf to the right as I continue to struggle with my sudden physical ailments. Bile is bubbling up from my stomach, and something is using a jackhammer on the inside of my head. If I didn't know better, I'd think I walked into a cemetery from the way I'm beginning to hear a faint voice.

"Both the discharge attendant and the transport company must sign the transfer log, April. It's audited every morning," Ricky says.

I nod mutely at him. It's the best I can do under the circumstances, as vertigo is threatening to make me sit down on the tile floor.

Ricky squints. "Are you all right?"

I offer him a smile I hope doesn't look too fake as I swallow the bitterness creeping up from my throat.

"You get used to it." Ricky steps past me and opens the door to my left. The garbled noise in my head becomes a woman's gravelly voice as if someone has tuned an analog radio to a station.

"Excuse me. There has been some sort of a mistake," the woman says.

I cross my arms as a bone-chilling cold flashes to my core. A freezing white fog rolls out of the walk-in cooler.

Ricky steps inside. He examines the multiple stainless-steel gurneys in the morgue. Most are empty, but for a handful with a mound of white plastic on top of them.

"This one is your patient, Walter," Ricky says. He separates the white plastic covering the body as he points to the man's face. Walter uncovers the lower half of the patient and double-checks the toe tag.

"All good, Ricky," Walter says.

"Excuse me," the voice calls to me as Ricky pulls Walter's gurney into the cooler.

My heart rate races, and it becomes impossible to breathe. My eyes dart from the left to the right as I see multiple mounds wrapped in white plastic bound loosely by white twine. The bodies are each on a gurney with a stainless-steel tray. They are meticulously organized along the wall of the giant cooler.

I don't care if anybody thinks I'm a wackadoodle now. I grab at the back of my head as another round of migraine pains flash through my brain.

"Excuse me. Miss, I'm talking to you."

I pivot to look at a gurney opposite where Ricky and Walter are working. I'm certain the voice is coming from the wrapped body on the gurney, second from the door on the left.

So much for no paranormal events. I walked right into this —literally. The spirit can feel my supernatural energy and is attracted to me. It is actively reaching out toward my energy signature.

The struggle not to run from the morgue is real. Of all the rotten luck in the world. Shane was right. From the description Ricky gave, this job is tailor-made for studying while receiving a paycheck. For anyone other than me.

"Ma'am. I know you can hear me," the gravelly voice says.

I try to convince myself I can push through this obstacle. I need to keep this job to have a chance at making it in Atlanta.

I avoid cemeteries like the plague. Specifically, because recent deaths or spirits of high energy levels that have remained behind will immediately sense me and talk incessantly.

It's not like I fault them. When you're dead, I suppose there are few folks you can talk to and ask for help. When you do find one, it's only natural you'd seek their assistance. If they ignored you,

you'd become louder and more belligerent. The squeaky wheel gets the grease and all.

That's exactly what's happening now. I have not responded to the woman, and I can hear the frustration and panic in her voice. That makes two of us who are panicked and frustrated.

I have always had some paranormal abilities, but until my twelfth birthday, they were minor. Then it changed quickly. An occasional moment of déjà vu or odd whispering voice in the wind suddenly turned into voices continually screaming at me in my head. The first few days, I thought I was going crazy until I talked to Mama about it.

At first, I told her I had headaches. But as we continued to talk, she unexpectedly asked if I ever heard anyone who wasn't alive.

Her question was the most relief-inducing thing I have ever heard in my life. Immediately I knew I wasn't alone.

Mama called Nana, and we drove out to her trailer in the woods. Nana is a self-professed animist. Everyone else calls her a witch. Either way, that day, she was my angel, as she instructed me on how to build partitions in my mind and block out the voices. I can never block them out completely, but it turns the volume way down to where most days I can ignore them, and some days I don't even notice them at all.

I pull the energy from the room to me. I hold as much of it compacted near my chest as I can muster. Then I compress it tightly around my sternum, concentrating on building partitions and quieting the voices. I can feel the barriers going up in my mind like a tall brick wall. The woman's voice grows quieter, one brick at a time.

"Hey, April, can you give us a hand?"

The distraction stops the progress in my mind, and the lady's gravelly voice begins to grow in volume again. I open my eyes. Walter and Ricky are looking at me oddly.

Great. There is no way I'll be able to look normal and build the much-needed partitions until we're done here.

I step into the cooler. Ricky gestures. "You get down there at the feet, and Walter and I will get the heavy half. We're going to slide Mr. Turley off the hospital gurney onto Walter's transport gurney."

Understand, right now I'd prefer to stick my hands in a hot Fry Daddy than grab Mr. Turley around the ankles. I can see the outline of his feet through the thin white plastic. White twine is tied snuggly at his knees. This is all obviously a test to see just how desperately April wants to stay in Atlanta.

I want to stay more than anything in the world. I reach out and grab hold of the man's legs.

It's night, and I'm walking on the sidewalk with two other young men. I'm holding a bottle in one hand and a cigarette in the other. The air is thick with humidity. I hear dogs barking in the distance.

Headlights shine from behind, and as I hear the car approaching, I turn and am blinded by the LED high beams. One of the guys I'm walking with grabs my arm and pulls me away from the road.

I resist momentarily as I stare at the red sedan. As it pulls level with me, my eyes adjust. Both passenger side windows are down, and my gut clenches.

Pistol barrels poke from the windows. I flinch. Before I drop to the ground, the gunfire reverberates in my head, followed by a burning sensation of hot metal rods being forced into my chest and puncturing my lungs.

Falling to my side, my head smacks the pavement—whitewall tires spin inches from my face. The smell of acrid smoke fills my nostrils, and the taste of blood dominates my mouth.

Chapter 11

"There she is." A young woman's face is inches from mine. I struggle to sit up, and she holds my shoulders. "Easy now. Let's take it slow. We don't want you to crack your head again."

Crack my head? What in the world is she talking about?

A man squats down next to the lady. He has red spiked hair and looks familiar.

"Are you alright, April?"

Ricky. His name is Ricky. I pull in a deep breath and survey my surroundings.

I wish I hadn't.

I'm still in the morgue. Worse, I'm sitting on the walk-in cooler floor, and I'm quite sure I was recently taking an un-planned siesta on the gray concrete.

Something burns my nostrils. I shake my head side to side. The young lady grimaces as she pulls something in her hand back toward her.

"Sorry, smelling salts. But they can help."

"I want to get up." Suddenly all I can think about is to get off this nasty floor.

Ricky moves toward me. "Jane, can you give me a hand getting her up?"

"Sure."

Putting their arms around me, they help me to my feet. What

precipitated my spontaneous nap is coming back to me. I look to the right, but Mr. Turley, as well as his ride, Walter, are gone. Oddly, the elderly woman's voice is quiet, too.

"I'm sorry," I croak.

"Don't be silly," Ricky says. "I'm just glad to see you're okay."

Jane pulls a thin flashlight from her pocket, then flashes the light in my right eye. I squint and jerk away. She holds my chin with her other hand and checks my left eye. "I don't know, Ricky. She doesn't have a concussion."

"Can you stay with me until I get her to the office? I'll feel better once she's sitting in a chair."

"Sure. That'll be a better place to check her out more completely anyway."

"I'm standing right here," I grumble.

"Sorry," Jane says. "You made us a little nervous. We were worried you struck your head on the tile when you took a tumble."

"Yeah, you just fell straight back. From the sound, I was afraid you cracked your skull open."

"At least you wouldn't have had to take me very far," I say.

Ricky and Jane laugh at my poor attempt at gallows humor. Jane walks me toward the office as Ricky locks the morgue.

I'm horrified I passed out like that. Ricky must think I'm some sort of weakling who faints at the sight of blood. Nothing could be further from the truth.

It sure would have been helpful though if Shane had given me a job description. If he told me I'd be releasing bodies to undertakers, I could've prepared myself and built the partitions in my mind strong enough to keep the voices at bay.

Who am I kidding? If Shane had told me the job was a morgue attendant, I would have told him, straight out, no. Being around dead folks and reigniting my paranormal abilities would have frightened me too much to even consider this job.

That would have been a mistake. Even at minimum wage, this job will easily cover my groceries and gas expenses in Atlanta. I still don't see a housing solution for when I must leave my apartment, besides joining a gym and sleeping in my car. Yet, I wasn't expecting this job that dovetails into my scheduling needs perfectly either. Something positive will come up on the housing front, too. I'm sure it will.

I do have to gain control of my abilities and block the voices. Easy peasy. I have done it before, and with so much on the line, I'll make it happen now.

Jane sits me down in the chair and does several tests I assume are cognitive. On the last one, she holds up three fingers and asks me, "How many fingers?"

"Six," I say.

Her brow furrows.

"I'm just kidding."

She slaps the side of my arm lightly. "Girl, don't even. Head trauma is nothing to be joking about."

"I assure you I come from an extensive line of hardheaded people. There is a greater chance of that concrete being cracked than me being hurt."

"Easy for you to say. You didn't see or hear you hit the floor like I did." Ricky scowls as he enters the office.

"Have you ever had incidents like this before?" Jane asks me.

Yes, but not the ones she's thinking of. "No. But I have not eaten today. If I were to guess, I experienced a low-blood-sugar episode." I hope Jane doesn't have the equipment with her to test my blood sugar.

Ricky gestures toward the door. "Then let's go get something to eat."

"I should probably get back to the ER," Jane says.

"You have your cell phone. They'll call you if they need you. Let me buy you an ice cream or something as a thank you," Ricky says.

"You don't have to. Besides, I should be getting back."

"Jane, don't make a grown man beg."

She flashes a bright white smile in contrast to her dark skin. "I suppose it wouldn't hurt. It will give me some more time to observe April and make sure she's well."

Geez, the awkward sexual tension is so thick in the air I can cut it with a knife. But it is sort of sweet. I'm glad I could facilitate it by passing out on the floor like a loser.

The three of us walk toward the building entrance and take the elevator to the second floor. The doors open just off a large cafeteria.

The low blood sugar was just an excuse, but now that we're at the cafeteria, I realize I'm starving. Hospital food, I have heard, isn't the best. So, my expectations are low. If I'm lucky, I'll find something I want to eat.

"The barbecue and the fried chicken are okay. Stay away from the hamburger steak. It'll sit in your stomach like a rock for a week," Ricky says.

"What you want is the chicken pot pie. They only serve it on Friday. It's your lucky day," Jane says.

"Yeah, I'm not much of a chicken pot pie fan," I say.

"Your loss. It's the best you will ever try," Jane says.

Since Jane woke me up from the dead, I decide I could at least buy a chicken pot pie on the side and give it a taste. For the main attraction, I go with barbecue pork, boiled cabbage, and black-eyed peas.

"Man, I am not looking forward to sharing an office with you today," Ricky says as we sit down.

"I have a steel-lined stomach. You have nothing to worry about."

"Famous last words," he says as he unwraps his ice cream Drumstick.

"So, how did you end up over at the morgue helping me out?" I ask Jane.

"Ricky called me and told me. We're slow over at the ER right now, so Dr. Lamont didn't mind letting me break free."

"I'm glad you were available. I'd hate to have been on that floor any longer than I was. It's giving me the heebie-jeebies just thinking I took a nap on it."

"I wouldn't have let you stay down long," Ricky says. "But I was concerned you might have hurt your neck, and I didn't want to move you until Jane checked you out."

I touch the back of my head to make sure there isn't a lump. The way Ricky is carrying on, you would think I fell down a flight of stairs instead. But there is no lump on my head, although my shoulders are sore.

"Do you really think it's because you hadn't eaten?" Ricky asks.

I am the world's worst liar. True story, I can't tell a believable lie face to face to save my life. I stare down at my cabbage as I answer, "Definitely." It was the only answer I could give Ricky. It's not like I'm going to tell him, "Oh, it was the reliving of Mr. Turley's last seconds on earth as he became a victim of a drive-by shooting that caused me to swan dive onto the concrete."

He sighs loudly. "Good. I have worked thirty days straight covering the open position, and I'm looking forward to having the next two days off."

The thought of being alone on the job the next two days slows my appetite. What if I have another episode but by myself in the cooler? Who would call for help?

The transporter would. I almost forgot that Walter, who seems to have disappeared, was with us.

"I'm glad you're getting a day off, too," I say.

"I was surprised to see on the new schedule I'm off the next two days," Jane says as she looks intently at her ice cream sandwich.

I wait impatiently for Ricky to make his move through the emotional door Jane left wide open for him. "I have an idea, Jane, how about we go for dinner and a show?" I almost say for him. If he were closer, I'd kick the living tar out of his shin right now.

The painful silent moment passes. I wonder if they are as tortured as I am watching their awkwardness.

Jane balls up the foil from her ice cream sandwich. "I better get back to the ER. Call me if you start feeling weird."

"I will," I say.

Ricky hops up from his chair, and I become hopeful he'll ask Jane out. He pulls up inches from her. "Thank you again for rushing over. I didn't know what to do."

"No worries. You can call me anytime." She stares at him with her large, dark eyes.

Ricky's white cheeks flush a rose color. "Thank you."

Jane pauses then exhales. "Thank you for the ice cream."

Ricky stares into her eyes. He appears hypnotized.

"Okay. Bye now." Jane turns away and walks out of the cafeteria. Ricky watches every step of her compact, shapely body until she disappears out the door.

"Why don't you ask her out?" I growl.

Ricky shakes his head as if coming out of a trance. "Jane?"

I roll my eyes. "Who else would I be talking about?"

He flushes a deeper shade of red, matching the color of his hair. "Oh, we're just friends. She would never go out with me."

Disgusted, I dive my fork into my chicken pot pie. "Well, those were not friend looks she was flashing you."

He scoffs. "No. You're mistaken."

"No, you're an idiot, and you can't read girls at all. If anyone should know the look she was giving you, it would be me. I have used it successfully many times. Of course, I never ran across anyone as clueless as you."

To accentuate my disdain for his cluelessness, I shove a large bite of chicken pot pie into my mouth. *Oh my gosh, this is delicious. Who knew? I love chicken pot pie.*

Chapter 12

As I'm entering Mr. Turley's information into the office logbook, the on-call cell phone rings. I stare at it on the desk and then look up at Ricky.

He gestures with his hand. "Well, aren't you going to answer it?"

I hesitate, not knowing what to expect, then I get over my nervousness and answer, "Metro Morgue, April speaking."

"Hey, this is Kendra up at ICU. I have a patient for you in room three forty-seven, West Tower."

I scramble to find a pen and paper. Ricky pushes a notebook toward me with a pen attached to it. We exchange smiles, and I transcribe the information. "Okay, we'll be there shortly."

"Thanks."

Ricky reads the notebook upside down from the other side of the desk. "Whew, the head trauma ICU is on the other side of the hospital. You're going to wish you wore tennis shoes."

"It's nothing but a thing. I wouldn't know how to walk in a pair of shoes that didn't have a heel." Forget tennis shoes. I wish I wore ballet slippers.

"Let's break out the Trojan Horse," Ricky says as he steps out of the office.

My curiosity almost gets the best of me. I want to ask Ricky what he means by Trojan Horse. But what's the point? He's about to show me, so I follow him to the morgue.

As he works the lock on the double door, I focus my attention on building partitions in my mind. It won't be as stable as I'd like, but hopefully, it'll do in a pinch. The doors open, and this time I'm not bowled over by the psychic energy. I feel it around me, but it's not permeating my mind and assaulting me.

"We keep the transport gurneys at the back during shift change. During your shift, you can leave one out in the foyer. It doesn't offend any of the transport folks."

Ricky pulls open the freezer door. I peer around the door, more cautious this time of the bodies inside.

I hear the faint voice from earlier, but the volume is less than ten percent of my previous foray into the freezer. I watch Ricky pull a big gurney with a plastic cover out of the freezer. I cringe at the height of the transport. From the looks of it, we'll have to pick the body up to place it on the transport unit rather than slide the body over.

Ricky pulls the gurney out of the foyer area and locks the double door as we exit. He hands me the keys. "All right, you've seen me open it twice. From here on out, they're yours."

"I think I can handle it."

"Did you grab the morgue phone?"

My stomach tightens. "That I did not."

He raises his eyebrows at me.

"I'll go get it."

"Hurry up. Those head trauma beds are in hot demand the closer we get to the weekend."

That makes no sense to me. Maybe it's some lame joke Ricky is making up to make me feel bad for holding up progress. I unlock the office door and retrieve our common cell phone.

Walking back toward the morgue, I decide to call Ricky on his jest. "Why would head trauma ICU beds be in higher demand on the weekend?" I look at him pointedly.

Ricky chuckles. "Hey y'all, watch this."

Darn it, he's right. I nod my head in agreement, and he laughs again as he pulls the gurney down the hall.

I'm not in the medical profession. Still, due to them being common lawsuits, I'm aware Georgia, like my home state of Alabama, ranks high in the number of per capita head injuries. I'm also mindful that these head injuries often occur right after an individual says, "Hey y'all, watch this." It's incredible what people will do to try to impress their friends.

We arrive at the elevator, and I hold the door while Ricky loads the gurney. He explains we must go up to the eighth floor to get to the West Tower, and then we'll have to take the elevator down to the third floor.

"Are you studying to be a doctor?"

Ricky's question catches me off guard. "No. I'm out of school. I finished law school."

Ricky leans sideways and shares an exaggerated shocked look. "Dang, girl. What are you doing here?"

I try not to grit my teeth. "Making a living like everybody else."

"I hear that. But it just surprises me. Is it hard to get a job as a lawyer?"

"Ask me in a month, and I'll let you know. I just started looking here in Atlanta."

"I got you. Do you have family in Atlanta?"

I frown and hope Ricky gets the message I don't want to talk this much about me. "No."

"Friends?"

Ricky is clueless. I forgot about that. "No, how about you?"

"Oh yeah, all my family is in Atlanta. Well, Cobb County. I commute in."

We come to the elevator in the West Tower. Ricky isn't kidding. The tiled concrete slab floors are killing my arches, and my Achilles tendons feel stretched beyond repair.

"Are you dating anyone?" Ricky asks.

I give up. Ricky will not get a clue and understand I don't want to tell someone I just met everything about me. I begin the game of batting his question back at him. "No, how about you?"

He blushes. "No. I'm not much of a ladies' guy."

Right. Like I hadn't already seen that firsthand. Ricky might be a considerate and friendly guy, but he's tone-deaf when it comes to women.

"How do you know Janet?" he asks.

"I don't. How do you know her?"

"My mom cleans her house twice a week. A couple of years ago, she mentioned to her I was interested in medical, and Doc suggested I work at the hospital and figure out if I do like it."

"And?"

He shrugs. "I like it a lot. But man are they talking about a lot of school time to be a nurse and even more if you want to be a doctor."

I must be careful not to speak my mind about colleges. When I review my student loan debt, I get angry as a wet hen about how much of the money was a waste. I was required to pay for seven years to finish my law degree. I can honestly say if all the fluff and useless classes were cut out, I would have completed it in three and a half years. Cutting my student loan in half compared to what I'm looking at would be extremely attractive.

We arrive at room three forty-seven. Ricky pushes open the door, and a nurse stands up at the nurse's station. "Y'all hold up."

Ricky acts as if this is normal, and we wait until the nurse is directly in front of us. "Y'all need to know this is a hepatitis C patient."

"I appreciate that," Ricky says.

"No worries." The nurse turns and walks back to her station.

I'm not positive what hepatitis C is, but I think it's a blood disease. I also think it's not something I want to catch.

"Here, put these on." Ricky hands me a pair of latex gloves and a mask. He must notice my apprehension, and he adds, "There is not much to it. We just have to be careful."

I know he means it to calm my nerves. But he failed.

I pull the gloves on and loop the elastic band of the mask over my head. As I feared, the deceased patient's bed is at least a foot below the top of our gurney. I steal my nerves and make sure all my partitions are up in my mind. I might as well get this over with. I reach under the patient's legs to help Ricky lift him.

"Hold up!"

I pause and stare at Ricky.

"You sure are impatient. Hold up just a second. The nurse said he had hepatitis C."

Ricky unties the string around the patient's neck and the one around his chest. He pulls the plastic wrap back, and I freeze at the sight of the pale, dead man inside the thin covering. Ricky peers in and pulls the wrapping back further as he examines the man's arms and chest.

"What are you doing?" I whisper.

"Checking for needles. They're supposed to remove them from the patients. If they're dead, you can be sure you don't want to be pricked by a needle that's been in their body. That goes triple when you've been warned they have a blood pathogen."

That makes sense, but it also causes me to want to ask why the nurses wouldn't be careful and remove all the needles. "Has that happened before?"

Ricky closes the plastic over the body and ties the string. "Not to me."

"Because you're careful."

"I'm no fool, no siree, I want to live to be a hundred and three," he sings the familiar cartoon tune as he ties the white twine back into place.

"I hope he's not as heavy as he looks," I say.

Ricky's head snaps up. He squints as he studies me, then laughs uncontrollably.

"What? What did I say?"

He sobers and points at our gurney. "Grab hold of the top and pull up."

I do as he asks, and the flat surface of the gurney pops off the two posts on my side. Ricky does the same, grabs the gurney top in the middle, and sets it against the wall. "That's the lid," he says as he points at the piece we just removed. "That's what Mr. Vernon's going to ride in." He gestures at the stainless-steel, raised-lip tray we exposed.

I'm staring at the contraption when he adds, "We'll be able to place the lid back on it once we get Mr. Vernon on the gurney. That way, we won't cause a panic as we're wheeling a dead body down the hallway. It's funny that you can walk by someone and they're not aware there is a dead body next to them."

"That's pretty cool."

"It is." He points to Mr. Vernon. "Well, get to it."

"By myself?"

Ricky nods his head. "You're going to be by yourself tomorrow and Sunday. It's time you learn how to do this solo."

I already figured I'd use my hips to pin the gurney against the patient's bed. By releasing the sheet the patient is on, I could easily slide him onto the gurney. That isn't the issue.

The hesitation came from my fear of what would happen when I touched Mr. Vernon. I don't want another flashback. I figure if I pass out again, Ricky will have to report the incident. Dr. Hamlin might believe I can't handle the job.

I pull the far side of the sheet edges over Mr. Vernon and then match the corners to the near side, as if I were folding the sheet out of the dryer. Then I pull firm and steady on the linen until Mr. Vernon slides neatly onto the stainless-steel tray.

"Wow. That's impressive how you figured that out on your own the first try."

"Thanks." It is simple physics, but having done it successfully without touching Mr. Vernon is a relief.

"Okay, so then we grab the cover, and the easiest thing to do is get one post in, and then you'll be able to feed the other three in."

I work the top into place and straighten the rectangular linen cover on the surface. Mr. Vernon is concealed completely.

"Shoot, I may just head on home. You have everything under control here." When I cut my eyes to Ricky, he laughs. "I'm just kidding. Let's get Mr. Vernon down to the morgue."

Three hours later, I'm more than ready to leave the hospital. Not because I have been working too hard, but because after Mr. Vernon, there was a three-hour quiet period. Ricky filled the time by asking me so many questions I finally asked him to be quiet and read something on his phone. I didn't want to be rude, but three hours is a long time to talk to anybody.

Driving home, I consider my good fortune. Shane is right; the job is perfect for studying. Sure, there are some glaring obstacles I'll have to navigate given my paranormal abnormalities. Still, I believe the job will be a blessing.

At a red light, I pick up my phone and dial Shane's number. I need to thank him for hooking me up.

He picks up on the first ring. "April?"

"Hi, did I catch you at an inconvenient time?"

"No, what's up?"

"I need to let you know I interviewed for the job at the hospital, and I got it, and I just finished my first shift. Well, half shift."

"Congratulations."

I can tell by his tone he's not at all surprised. "I appreciate you putting in the good word with Dr. Hamlin for me. She hired me on the spot, and like you said, I think it will be perfect for me to study most days."

"Good. I know it will help Janet, too. She has a tough time keeping a full staff."

"That seems odd, considering it's perfect for anyone needing to study."

"Not everybody wants to deal with dead bodies."

His comment doesn't sit well with me. "Hey, they're people too, or at least they were a few minutes before the nurses call the morgue."

"I didn't say I have a problem. I said there are a lot of people that do."

"Well, I want to tell you thank you."

"You're more than welcome."

The silence on the line cues me; it's time to say goodbye. But I'm not ready to just yet. Before I can think of something else to say, Shane asks, "What are you doing for dinner?"

My heart skips a beat, and I feel flushed all over. "I was just gonna cook some mac and cheese or something."

"Let me buy you dinner."

"No, Shane. You've already done too much."

"Then you buy mine."

I pause as I try to calculate in my head how much money I could free up for dinner for two and where we can go.

"I'm kidding. But we do need to celebrate, and I don't have anyone to eat dinner with tonight," he says.

"You sure do use that excuse a lot."

"It's not an excuse. It's the truth, and if I have an option, I'd rather eat dinner with someone than not."

My mind goes back to my nap on the morgue floor earlier today. "The thing is, I have to take a shower first."

"Heck yeah. I don't want to be eating dinner with some chick who's been handling dead people before she takes a shower."

"You know you really should be more respectful of the dead."

"Honey, you don't even know. I'll pick you up at eight at your place."

"I didn't say I was going."

"See you at eight. Bye, now."

I can't believe Shane hung up on me. I want to be peeved that he did, but his antics were humorous and slightly flattering.

If I can get the "where to live cheaply" part of the equation solved, I have a real shot at making it in Atlanta. I'm convinced I'll find employment at a firm. It's just a numbers game. I need to keep contacting as many people as possible.

It's funny. Just this morning, I had to beat back the idea of moving home until I earned my license. But now, with the lifeline of a job to pay for my groceries and gas, and provide time for studying, I wouldn't even consider going home.

Besides, I'd be lying if I said I wasn't highly curious where the

Shane relationship is going. I'm not sure if it's love, but there is something about him that makes every inch of my skin tingle when I get around him. If it's not love, it's some extra heavy-duty lust.

Chapter 13

Typically, I don't bother with mascara. My lashes are naturally long and full. Still, I have a few extra minutes before eight and am applying it to my lashes when the doorbell rings—my stomach tingles. I shake my head as I walk to my door. I have got to get control of these feelings. It's not normal for me to be this into a guy I barely know.

I open the front door. Shane smiles at me, and I lose control of my emotions again. Is this what love feels like?

"Well don't you look beautiful," Shane says.

"Thank you." I gather my purse, step out, and lock the door behind me. "You look pretty sharp yourself."

"Shucks, I bet you tell all the guys that."

"Only the ones I eat dinner with."

Shane stops on the passenger side of a small, two-door coupe with wide tires. "How many guys are you eating dinner with?"

"It's not proper to ask a lady that."

Shane opens the passenger door. "I'm trying to get a feel for how many guys I'm up against if I decide to ask you out for dinner again."

"If?" I raise my eyebrows before I get into his car. I practically fall into the passenger seat because it's so low to the ground.

He grins as he shuts the door. I watch him intently as he walks in front of the car and gets in on the driver's side.

"Do you like Mexican?" he asks as he starts the car.

"Does a cat have climbing gear?"

"Yes, they do." He cuts his eyes at me. "Buckle up."

La Siesta is a small, family-owned restaurant at the end of our street. The hostess sits us at the last available booth when we arrive.

"Do you want a margarita or a beer?"

Tempting, but I shake my head no.

Shane picks up the saltshaker and holds it over the tortilla chips. "To salt or not to salt."

I giggle. "Definitely salt."

He shakes salt liberally over the chips then dunks half a chip in the salsa. "Did you like it?"

"The job?"

"Yeah."

I shrug. "Not really. I mean, to your point, moving dead people isn't most folks' dream job, but I'm not doing it as a career. It's just a job. Plus, there is a lot of downtime, which is perfect for studying. For that reason, I love the job."

"Good." He rests his elbows on the table and props his chin on his laced fingers. Shane stares at me until I become self-conscious.

"Do I have something on my face?"

"Happiness. It becomes you."

I have another one of those full-body heat flashes. I'd kick myself if I could. I'm acting like a middle schooler with a crush. "Tell me, Shane, how is it that you don't have a girlfriend?"

"Did I say I don't have a girlfriend?"

"Well, you haven't mentioned one."

"Seems like it would be an odd thing for me to mention if you weren't asking."

"Does it?"

Shane raises his eyebrows then looks down at the menu. "So should I deduce you don't have a boyfriend?"

"You don't have to make it sound like I'm defective," I say.

"You want some cheese? I want some cheese." Shane raises his hand and makes eye contact with our waiter.

We've only known each other for a few days, but I'm already wondering what my relationship is with Shane. I'm becoming concerned that I'm way more into him than he is me. Not to sound conceited, but that would be a first, and I'm not sure how to manage a relationship with that dynamic.

There is also a part of me that thinks Shane is involved with a girl. A girl he loves very much, and he's just charitable to me because I am in need. If that's true, I'll be crushed. It would make me beyond pathetic.

Why? Because it means I am a charity case, which I don't care to be. Ever. That would signal to me I have hit rock bottom.

"What are you going with?"

Shane's voice pulls me out of the hamster wheel that is my mind. It's for the best. All I'm doing is playing a game of he loves me, he loves me not, minus the flower petal pulling.

I run my finger along the menu as if I have been studying it all along. "I'm thinking about the burrito with mole sauce."

"Not bad. Do you like chimichangas?"

"Yes."

"Just a suggestion, but I think their chimichangas are better than their burritos." He tosses a chip into his mouth.

I set the menu down. "I'll give it a try."

"Tell me the details. What shift were you assigned, and did she offer you enough of an hourly wage to make a difference?"

Darn it. I knew I'd forgotten something. I can't believe I took a job and I don't know my hourly wage. "I have twelve-hour shifts on the weekend. And two eight-hour shifts during the week to make my forty."

The waiter brings the cheese sauce to our table; Shane pulls it closer to us. "That's nice. It should leave a lot of hours for you to interview when you're not studying."

"Yes, it worked out better than I could've hoped."

"See, April. The universe is a friendly place."

Daddy, like his father, and his grandfather before him, is a Freemason. I have heard the statement before and wonder about the men in Shane's family.

Believe me, I try to defer to Daddy's opinion of the world. He's explained to me, people will be and events will transpire according to my expectations. Armed with that knowledge, I try my best to believe the universe truly is a friendly place. The only problem is, deep down inside of me, I think my entire being is built around a kernel that believes most people have a hidden agenda. If I want something, I'll have to fight for it.

Our waiter comes back, and we order.

"You've never told me what you do for a living. I hope you don't take offense, but does being a mover pay that well?"

Shane grins. "I'm not a mover. Yes, I was helping the other day. My friends have a company specializing in document transport and destruction for Redstone and occasionally for the FBI. He had a last-minute contract with the FBI to transport all the documents and computers from MLJ to the FBI storage facility in Huntsville. The problem was half of his usual movers had all gone down to the coast for a weeklong fishing trip. He asked me if I could help. I was available."

I twirl my hand. "And your real job is?"

"I'm sorry. I thought you knew. I work with Dr. Hamlin at the hospital."

"Do you work at the morgue, too?"

"No. The morgue is just a small part of what Dr. Hamlin is director of. I'm, for lack of a better term, one of her assistants."

Shane dips another chip, coating it in cheese, and pops it into his mouth. He looks toward the kitchen, and I know the conversation is over.

One thing I have learned quickly with Shane—when Shane is done with a line of questioning, he'll give you ample clues that there will be no further discussion.

The thing is, he hasn't told me anything. I barely know any more now than when we started the conversation.

I'm about to press him for more details when his phone rings.

He picks it up and grimaces. "I'm sorry, I'll have to take this."

"Sure."

"Hey, Pops, what's up?" He squints his eyes and covers his free ear. "She left?"

The waiter appears with our meals and sets them on the table.

"I don't understand. She left? Is she coming back?"

If I could make myself disappear right now, I would. It sounds like the conversation Shane is having is with some family member who's having marital issues. Not a conversation I need to be hearing.

"And she didn't say she was coming back? Pop, it's kind of important to know who's staying with you tonight."

The chimichanga is beautiful and smells even better. My mouth is watering, but I don't want to be rude and start eating before Shane.

"No. Absolutely not. I'll be there shortly. Don't you go anywhere." Shane hangs up.

"Is everything all right?"

He rolls his eyes. "Far from it. I'm sorry, but I'm going to have to leave. Family emergency."

My spirits sink. I was enjoying our time together and was looking forward to the meal. "I understand."

Shane raises his hand and again catches the waiter's eye. "There is no way you can understand."

Something about the way Shane said that tweaks me. "Try me. What's going on."

"I need this to go, please. A two-enchiladas dinner to go, too." After giving the instructions to the waiter, he turns his attention back to me. "I have guardianship of my grandfather. If I were a responsible man and had the intestinal fortitude he and my father have always exhibited, I would put him in a retirement community. But I'm a pushover, and I'm allowing him to stay in the home he and my grandmother built forty years ago. The only problem is, he constantly runs off the caregivers I hire."

"Why?"

Shane raises his eyebrows. "Why do they leave, or why does he run them off?"

I shrug. "I suppose both."

"They leave because he can be a hard-headed jerk when he wants to be." Shane exhales. "He's been battling stage four cancer for the last year, and it makes him meaner than he used to be. And he runs them off because he thinks he doesn't need them."

"Does he need them?"

Shane frowns. "Twenty-three and a half hours out of the day, no. But the half-hour he's in full dementia, especially considering he lives on the lake, yes, he needs a caregiver. I couldn't live with myself if something happened to him."

"What about the rest of your family?"

"All that's left is my dad and mom. They live up in Virginia. Dad is stationed up there."

Funny, I'm learning more in the last five minutes about Shane than I learned the previous five days. "Can I go with you?"

Shane's eyes open wide. "Why would you want to do that?"

"To meet your pop."

"You want to meet Pop?" Shane's frown turns into a lopsided grin. "I don't think you know what you're asking."

Pointing toward the kitchen, I say, "I assume the enchiladas are for him, and you're boxing your dinner so you can eat with him. I'll just have them put mine in a to-go box too, and we can all eat together like an ad hoc family."

"You don't have to do that. I'll just drop you off at your apartment on the way."

There is no point in arguing right now. I still need to get my dinner put in a to-go box, and I'll plead my case once we're in Shane's car.

I'm a firm believer if you want to really know somebody, you need to meet their family. A lot of things can be explained about a person by meeting their relatives. Heck, anyone who spent a little time with mine would fully understand where my quirkiness comes from.

We get in Shane's car with two bags, one with his and Pop's meal and one with mine. "I'm really sorry this happened. The timing is horrible."

"It'll be fun. I haven't had a sit down with the family in a few weeks."

Shane laughs. "You're not gonna let it drop, are you?"

"Nope."

"All right." He shakes his head. "But don't say I didn't warn you."

Chapter 14

We head north out of Atlanta. The sun is still bright, but I'm starting to think that I have made a mistake. I must be at work by seven a.m., and it just occurred to me I don't have a ride back to my apartment if Shane stays at his pop's.

This is the first time I have seen Shane aggravated. Since I'm only adding to his frustration by insisting on eating dinner with them, I remain quiet. I'll figure out my transportation issues later.

Shane takes a phone call. It sounds like the agency responsible for the caregiver who left Shane's grandfather by himself. I'm glad I wasn't on the receiving end of that phone call. Shane is one of those folks who can make you feel like they're cussing you out while being polite and using perfect language.

We take a turn in a small town called Flowery Branch. Weaving through tall pines that remind me of home, I catch glimpses of the lake through the trees and an occasional older large home. It's the first time I have seen something in Atlanta that puts my mind at ease.

Shane turns up a cul-de-sac and pulls into the drive of a rustic A-frame at the end of the court. "La casa de papá," he says as he puts the car in park. Grabbing both bags, he exits the vehicle.

I have no choice but to get out and follow him as quickly as possible. He opens the front door without even knocking, and I follow him in.

"Pop!"

I stand just inside the foyer and scan the open floor plan. I can see the kitchen and what must be the den. To the right, I see a small hallway that I assume leads to the bedrooms. The whole decor of the home is boomer bachelor. The only feminine items I see in the living area are a few figurines on top of a bookshelf and an antiquated entertainment center. They're covered in half an inch of dust.

"Pop!"

I hear a sliding glass door and then see Shane crossing in front of the bay window. There is a porch that wraps around the back of the house. I decide to follow Shane.

As I step out of the house onto the porch, Shane marches across a cobblestone path toward a boathouse at the water's edge. I grin as I see a man sitting in an Adirondack chair at the edge of the dock. I have never met the man, but I'm going to venture a guess that it's Pop.

Hustling down the porch steps, I make my way across the lawn. I hear Shane as I approach the dock.

"What do you think you're doing?" he asks.

"Watching the sunset."

"Don't be smart with me. I can't be running out here every other day because you've run another caregiver off."

I slow my pace as I reach the dock. This is not the proper conversation to get in on.

"You know, that's the smartest thing I have heard you say in a while," Pop says. "If you quit sending them out here, you wouldn't have to keep coming out. I have been taking care of myself for seven decades now, son. I don't need a nursemaid."

"That makes absolutely no sense."

"Humph." The older man takes a drag on his stubby cigar.

"And I told you, no cigars."

"Please. I'm going to be dead any day. I might as well go

happy."

"You need to stop that nonsense. What happened this time? Did you get mad because she wouldn't let you smoke, or did she not let you have your afternoon bourbon."

"Lulu didn't like her. So, I ran her off."

"You ... what! Blast it, Pop. Are you trying to make me miserable?"

"I don't have to. You do that to yourself naturally."

It isn't my place, but I know how sometimes these family arguments can metastasize into something more significant if you don't cut them short. I step forward and introduce myself. "Sir, I'm Shane's friend April." I extend my hand, and Pop tucks his cigar under a finger against the tumbler of amber liquor to free his right hand as he stands.

"Pleased to meet you, miss." His blue eyes are alert as his stare locks eyes with me and he shakes my hand. "Please call me John Michael." He continues to hold my hand and looks at Shane. "Glad to see you finally took some time to live and get you a girl, boy. A mighty pretty one, too."

Shane closes his eyes and exhales. "She's a friend, Pop."

He smiles as he releases my hand, looking at me while speaking to Shane. "Right."

"We really are just friends," I say to John Michael.

He sits back down in his chair. "I have to tell you that's very disappointing."

"What's disappointing is I had a long day at work, and now I'm going to have to wait a few hours out here because they don't have anyone else to send."

"Good. Tell them not to send anyone," John Michael says as he waves his cigar.

Shane starts to say something and then closes his mouth and eyes. It looks like he's doing yoga in his mind. When he opens his eyes, his face is back to the easy-going Shane I have become accustomed to. "Listen, Pop, I bought you a couple enchiladas. Come on back up to the house. Let's eat."

John Michael raises the tumbler in his hand. "I'm good."

"You need to eat something."

"And I told you I'm not hungry."

"What if I tell you I'll come to watch the Braves game with you Sunday night?"

John Michael purses his lips then points at me. "Is she coming with you?"

"No, she's working Sunday."

"That's disappointing."

I sense they're about to get into another argument when John Michael stands. "But it's the best offer I have had so far."

Following the two men to the house, I scan the yard. For a lake house, the lot is considerable, approaching an acre. I can also tell that there were numerous flowerbeds and nature areas around clusters of trees at one time. It isn't a jungle, but everything has an overgrown and slightly neglected look to it. The only things that look well maintained are the dock and boathouse. They're in better shape than the rustic A-frame home in terrible need of re-staining.

"You didn't get the enchiladas with that black or green sauce, did you?" John Michael complains.

"No, sir, it's the red sauce."

"Good."

John Michael takes a seat at the kitchen table. Shane unpacks the three meals and turns the oven on.

"Where's the silverware?" I ask.

Shane points. "Last drawer on the left."

I find the forks and carry them to the dinette table. I make a beeline to the refrigerator in the hope there are a few bottled waters inside.

Putting the three aluminum containers on an oven pan to warm in the oven, I see Shane stop and watch my search. I try to ignore him, but he's making me self-conscious.

"What are you looking for?"

"Bottled water?"

"Sorry. You might find some soda in there. He'll put a drop of Coke in his bourbon occasionally."

"Bottled water, humph," John Michael grunts. "Only a rube would buy bottled water. They charge so much for plastic and water; it would be cheaper to drink gasoline."

I close the fridge. "I'm good."

Shane opens the cabinet to his left and hands me two glasses. "The ice and water dispenser on the fridge work. If you're worried, I change the filter regularly."

Shane must have a bit of psychic himself, as that's precisely why I hadn't already used them. There is nothing worse than refrigerator water when the filter hasn't been changed in a couple of years. "Thanks," I say as I take the glasses from him.

"Would you like to explain yourself, Pop?"

"About what?" he says as he lifts his cigar to his mouth.

"There is no smoking in the house." Shane's voice cracks. "We talked about this."

John Michael wags his nubby cigar at Shane. "You talked about it incessantly. I didn't agree to anything. Besides, it's not been lit for hours."

Shane leans against the kitchen counter with his arms braced. He tucks his head in what I gather to be a prayer for strength and patience. As his body begins to shake, I realize he's struggling to contain his laughter.

I find it humorous too, but not for the same reasons as Shane. I'm highly surprised Shane's grandfather is a card-carrying curmudgeon. Given Shane's demeanor, I'd have expected him to be sensitive, likely an artist with a high sexual charisma quotient.

"You two really aren't dating?" John Michael directs his question to me.

"No, sir." I lean my back against the counter next to Shane as I answer.

"Are you married or engaged?"

His question makes my cheeks heat. "No, sir. I'm single."

John Michael squints his eyes. "Are you into the girls?"

"Pop!" Shane twists around. "What's the matter with you?"

He turns his hands over. "What? It's just a question. It's not like I have a problem with it."

Shane runs his hands through his hair. "Man, you're killing me."

"Oh, for Pete's sake." John Michael exhales. "I'm sorry if I offended you, young lady. I might not be up on all the current social codes. I assure you I didn't mean anything by it."

I'm struggling not to laugh. If I do, I'm afraid Shane will blow a gasket. "We're good, sir."

"See, she doesn't mind. You shouldn't be getting offended for other people, son."

"And you wonder why I don't bring visitors by."

"I do. It seems like you would want to share your wonderful Pop with more of them." The older man grins and takes a sip of bourbon.

I can't help myself. "I know. I practically had to beg him to bring me by to visit you tonight."

"I'm certainly pleased you did, young lady. But tell me, why is it that you two are just friends."

"Pop!"

"No. It's okay, Shane." I'd like an answer to that question too. Although John Michael is asking the wrong person. "We just met. I only recently moved to Atlanta."

"I see."

"Back on topic," Shane says. "What happened with the care-giver?"

"Son, I'm the one who's getting old, but you're the one who is either hard of hearing or forgetful. I already told you Lulu didn't like her."

"Geez, Pop." Shane shakes his head as he opens the oven.

"Who is Lulu?" I ask.

"I'll tell you later," Shane says.

"Lulu is Shane's aunt." John Michael squints in Shane's direction. "But some people have a problem believing she exists."

"We're not doing this anymore," Shane says as he puts a potholder down and John Michael's enchiladas on top of it. "Watch it. It's hot."

There is a story there, I'm sure. Still, where before their antics were good-natured ribbing, there is some underlying sharp-edged animosity about Lulu. My insane level of curiosity almost overrides my manners, causing me to probe the scab further. Luckily, Shane sets my chimichanga in front of me.

"Thank you," I say.

"I just hope you have not lost your appetite because of the Spanish Inquisition you're being subjected to."

"It doesn't bother me. If you ever meet my family, you'll understand I have been trained well."

I turn my attention to John Michael. "So, what was it you didn't like about today's helper?"

"It would be easier to say what I did like."

He doesn't continue, so I ask, "What *did* you like about her?"

"Not a darn thing."

I attempt not to crack a grin for Shane's sake. I know I don't need to encourage John Michael.

"You better find something to like about the one they send Monday, Pop. I have that certification up in Cincinnati, and I'll be gone all week. I can't take care of you if you run someone else off."

"I didn't run anybody off," John Michael grumbles.

Shane sits down with his meal. "You told her she was a stupid, fat cow!"

"I did not"—John Michael wrinkles his face—"I said nothing of the sort."

"Why in the world would the agency lie to me, Pop?"

"Well, they did. They are a bunch of liars." He cuts his eyes to me. "I called her a dull, obese sloth. She probably wasn't bright enough to know what a sloth was, although she could've looked it up on that phone she never got her nose out of."

Shane raises his fork. "And the truth comes out. When will you come to terms with the fact cell phones aren't going away?"

"They're from the devil. It makes me glad I am going away."

Shane shakes his head and ignores John Michael's last statement. He focuses on his meal.

I'm sure Shane feels John Michael is merely playing up his illness with all the "dropping from the list of the living" barbs. I know it's common for some people to focus on their disease for attention. Still, when I shook John Michael's hand, his pain leeched to me temporarily. I was shocked at the level of pain I felt that racks his body. It's incredible the man can be civil at all. If he's not close to death, I'm sure he might fondly think of it as a release from his agony.

Shane said that his illness had made John Michael meaner. I'm sure that is true. But just like his grandson, besides the icky, oily coating of pain, he has a golden core that leaps forward to the touch.

There has never been genuine meanness in John Michael. That's why Shane will drive an hour to visit and take care of him no matter how it interferes with his evening. Love calls all back home.

I can't fathom the ache Shane must be feeling. It must be heartbreaking to watch someone you love disintegrate a little more each day and discuss their imminent passing so freely.

Guessing my granny is a few years older than John Michael and my nana a few years younger. How fortunate am I both are in vibrant and in excellent health? The thought of witnessing their deterioration like Shane has to watch John Michael is disturbing and not something I want to dwell on.

"Pop, are you not going to eat?" Shane asks.

"I appreciate you bringing it, but I don't have much of an appetite tonight," John Michael says as he takes another sip of bourbon.

"We might need to up your pain medication?"

John Michael lifts his tumbler. "I don't mind if I do."

"I mean the one the doctor prescribed."

"I don't like the way they make me feel."

Shane opens his mouth to argue and then closes it. His nose twitches as if he's about to sneeze. Rising, he picks up his plate and turns from us quickly. "We still should check in with them tomorrow and see if they can give you a different medication."

A lot is going on in this room. And a lot more that's not being said. I decide it's an excellent time to interject myself. "So, you're a Braves fan, John Michael?"

He shrugs. "I try to be, but most years, they're a bunch of bums. Nothing like the team in the early nineties. Now that was a team."

Shane laughs as he picks up my empty tray and John Michael's two enchiladas. "Here we go again."

"There has never been a team to have a lineup of pitchers like the Braves in the nineties. It's a fact, Shane," John Michael says.

I have heard this tale at least a hundred times myself from my daddy and uncles. To listen to them talk, the Atlanta Braves put together a dynasty. I made a mistake once of asking Daddy why they only won one World Series. I'll never make that mistake again.

True to form of every Braves fan over the age of fifty, John Michael recounts the glory days of Smoltz, Maddux, and Glavine. I like baseball a lot, but having heard the story so often, it usually is tiresome. The way John Michael's pain fades from his face as he describes the pennant race of '92, the story is captivating tonight.

"Listen, I have got this new channel Shane got me called new flicks."

"Netflix, Pop."

"Stupid name, but it's got some great shows. There is one show I started watching they tell me is filmed here in Atlanta. Imagine that." He shrugs. "It's a knockoff from *Dawn of the Dead*, but it's a terrific version. You've got to watch it with me."

"Pop, April has to be at work early in the morning."

"You know I think I've heard of that show." I have watched all episodes of *The Walking Dead*, but it wouldn't hurt me to watch a show with John Michael if it would make him happy. "I can stay and watch one episode."

John Michael hops out of his seat with a speed that surprises me. "I'll go pull it up."

As John Michael leaves the room, Shane turns to me. "April, you really don't have to do this."

"Come on, Shane. I couldn't exactly tell him no. Besides, if it makes him happy, I can watch an episode of a stupid TV show."

"Thank you."

His sincerity catches me off guard as I'm standing, and I snort a laugh. "Whatever."

He stands, and we walk into the den together. John Michael is pressing buttons on the remote furiously.

"I can't get this stupid thing to work."

"Here, let me try." Shane holds his hand out.

"I forgot my water. I'll be right back," I say as I walk to the kitchen.

Being at John Michael's helps me understand Shane's earlier comments. It's true his grandfather is a handful and needs assistance. Yet I can also tell John Michael, in his prior years, was an independent, self-sufficient man and wouldn't take well to having someone overtly helping him. Especially if they appeared to be bored or put out by the task.

I pick up my water and turn to go back into the den. The entity on the ceiling freezes me in my tracks. I take note of the smoke gathering at the top of the kitchen ceiling in the far corner. It undulates in and out of focus in a manner dissimilar from natural smoke.

Was it there earlier? I don't remember seeing it, and I find it hard to believe I wouldn't have noticed if it were in the kitchen when we were eating.

Besides, I can feel the slight tingle of the entity's energy. It's weak, and there is no voice.

I'm careful to only look at it in my peripheral vision. It vacillates in the corner. Then, without warning, it trails across the edge of the ceiling and goes through a door to the kitchen's right, offset from the sliding glass door.

Odd.

Shane seems to have tamed the remote control and is selecting an episode. "Hey, guys, what's that door off of the kitchen?" I ask.

John Michael cuts his eyes to me. "The master bedroom."

"Is this the one?" Shane asks.

"Ah, just let it roll. If I have seen it already, we can jump to the next one," John Michael says as he sits down in a recliner.

I sit down on the sofa close to John Michael. Once Shane has the show running, he sits down "friend" close to me. That's okay; I'm wearing him down. He'll have his arm around me in no time.

Chapter 15

In the middle of a super gory zombie battle, heads are decapitated, blood of the thick and black style flies across the screen liberally, and the loudest snoring ever starts up. John Michael's mouth is wide open, and he's making the gosh-awfullest sound I have ever heard.

"Is he okay?" I ask Shane.

Shane laughs. "It's the bourbon. He always snores when he drinks."

I start giggling. "I don't think I can hear the show."

"Nah. I have seen this one anyway."

"Me too," I say.

"I need to get him in bed." He lifts the TV controls and turns the TV off.

When the noise of the zombie battle goes off, John Michael wakes up with a start in his recliner. "What, what. What's the matter?"

"Show's over. Time to go to bed, Pop."

John Michael yawns and lets the footrest of his recliner down. "Yeah, I'm beat."

Shane looks at me. "Can you give me a minute to get him in bed?"

I shrug. "It's not like I can go anywhere."

"Right. I forgot about that." Shane puts his arm around Pop

and leads him toward the kitchen. "I'll give you my keys in a minute."

Keys to his car? Surely he means something else. Nobody gives their car keys to someone they met only a few days earlier.

Their steps become quieter with distance, and I hear the master room door open. I walk back to the kitchen to get another look at the ceiling.

I peek my head over the threshold into the kitchen. Nope, still gone.

Of course, the entity had such a weak energy signature, it may have just dissipated. I have a desire to go into the master bedroom and see if it's in there, but my curiosity will have to deal with not knowing.

Shane comes through the door and pulls it closed. "He's out like a light."

"Is he okay?"

Waving his hand, Shane says, "Oh yeah, he's fine. He'll only sleep for four or five hours. That's about tops for him. Of course, if he didn't take two naps a day, he probably could sleep through the night."

"Something tells me you're not going to get him to heed that advice."

"Right after the cigar and the bourbon, I'm sure." Shane reaches into his pants pocket and pulls out his keys. He removes a key from the ring. "You can drive yourself home?"

He holds the keys out to me, and I hesitate. "That leaves you without a vehicle."

"Pop has a pickup truck and a car in the garage. I keep the garage locked in case he decides to go for a road trip. You can just park mine at the apartment, and I'll get it later."

I take the key from him. "But then you'll have an extra vehicle at the apartment."

"I'll ask a friend to follow me back one day, or who knows, maybe I can even bribe a girl to come to dinner tomorrow night, and then I can drive her home."

"I suppose stranger things have happened."

He walks me to the front door. "I know. A good rule of thumb is never to be surprised."

"What are you going to do about his caregiver?"

"I'm not sure yet. I'll call a new agency tomorrow and see what they can arrange."

"So, you're really gonna be gone next week?"

He flashes an uber-sexy smile. "Miss me already?"

"If I did, would it matter?"

"It always matters." He opens the door and steps out to the porch. I follow. "Again, thank you for being so sweet to him. I haven't seen him that energized in ages."

"Stop with that. I had a fun time, too."

Shane opens the driver's door. "Well, you definitely have a friend for life. I have never seen him take to anybody that quick."

"Really?" I say as I fall onto the low seat.

"Seriously. It usually takes Pop forever to warm up to somebody. You drive safe now."

I smile. "I won't hurt your precious car."

I'm not worried about the car," Shane says as he shuts the door. He steps back from the vehicle and watches me adjust the mirrors and the car seat before entering my apartment address into my phone's GPS app.

I start the car and wave at him. He waves back, and I pull out of the drive.

Exhaling, I let out the pent-up frustration in my body as I turn onto the street and head back to Atlanta. If I had any doubt at the start of the evening, I've got my answer now loud and clear.

Shane and I are just friends. Really good, "I'll let you borrow my car" kind of friends. But friends all the same.

I have had guy friends my entire life. My best friend in high school was Jacob Hurley, and then Marvin in law school. In both cases, we were so tight, people thought we were a couple. But there were never any romantic inclinations on our part.

The only thing is, in the case of Shane, I'm really interested in him. That's not something that complicated my past guy friend relationships.

Sadness washes over me, and for a second, I'm afraid I'll cry. Not that it matters. No one's in here to see me, but it's stupid. I have so many things I need to worry about right now. The last thing I need is to get upset about a non-relationship.

Instead, I should be grateful I have someone who's helped me make the transition to Atlanta. That, more than any romantic inclinations I have toward Shane, is the most important thing right now. He's helped me figure out how to get out of my lease, and he's hooked me up with a job that will fill my needs. That's a good friend indeed.

But I'd be lying if I said I didn't want more.

As I take the on-ramp onto the highway, I take a deep breath and push all those troubling thoughts away. I can't control how Shane feels about me. As much as I want to think about how I can wear him down in time and he'll come to love me, it's best if he doesn't. I deserve more than a man who settles on me. I shouldn't want a man who must be convinced I'm someone he wants to have as a partner. That would be a bad foundation for a long-term relationship.

Though it might be good fun for a short-term relationship.

Stop it, April. Just let it go.

I'm a little nervous about tomorrow. Even though the job seems easy and straightforward, I must believe a few hours of instruction can't possibly be enough training.

My mind is racing, and I turn on the radio in hopes of finding some distraction. I scan through the FM dial twice and turn it off.

The epiphany hits me like a light bulb going off for a comic caricature. John Michael needs a caregiver, and I need a place to stay.

No, that's stupid, April. You don't even know those people. Shane wouldn't consider the arrangement.

He said John Michael took to me, and he usually doesn't

warm up to people. Besides, I like him, I understand him.

No, the scheduling wouldn't work. I wouldn't be able to be there when I'm working my shift or interviewing. Shane said John Michael needs constant care.

Too bad. For a second, I thought I had my housing issue figured out and a way to help Shane. If it had worked, between that and the job at the morgue, I could quickly finish my licensing process and kick my interviews into high gear. Plus, I might be repaying Shane a little for all his help.

Oh well, something will happen on the housing front. It must.

Chapter 16

Oh my gosh. I'm so bored. I want to claw my face. I brought a law book to effectively use the downtime. Still, I never expected to study the entire twelve-hour shift.

I check the time on my phone again. I have been at work for four hours now, and nothing. There have been no incoming or outgoing patients, making it like I'm stuck in a mandatory study hall with no one to keep me company.

At least lunch will be coming up soon. That'll be a nice distraction.

I suppose after that, if the slow pace continues, I can go for a walk around town. I have the morgue cell phone with me. It's not like I'm chained to the desk.

The morgue phone rings. I stare at it in disbelief. Whoa. Talk about talking it up.

"Metro morgue, how can I help you?" I say as I answer the phone.

"Hi, this is Edith over at the emergency room. We have a patient for you."

A sense of excitement surges through me as I go on my first call. I run through my mind all the different things Ricky showed me yesterday. I unlock the morgue doors and open the walk-in cooler to pull out one of the transport gurneys.

Marjorie, the young nursing student who covers the third

shift of the morgue on the weekends, briefed me when I arrived for work. We have two patients who will be released today. Other than them, the large walk-in cooler is empty save for the vacant transport gurneys.

Today, unlike yesterday, there is no paranormal energy emanating from the patients. The elderly woman from yesterday is gone. The two remaining patients appear to have passed calmly to their next state of being, making a clean jump across the veil.

The veil is what Nana calls the separation between the living and the dead. Her explanation to me in the past is the veil is not permeable for most living or deceased. The living remain on their side, and the dead on the other.

Some folks have the "gift" of their veil being fragile and, in some cases, porous. This allows them to slip from one side to the other. I'm one of the few lucky people in the world affected by this affliction. However, my veil isn't just porous. I'd describe it as a tattered sheet you can drive a bus through.

In the case of Ms. Crenshaw, the elderly woman from yesterday, her spirit simply resisted moving across the veil. Once she comes to peace with her death, she'll slide through the veil. When she does, she'll remain on that side. Unless, of course, Ms. Crenshaw has a thin veil, too.

Without the paranormal subterfuge, the morgue is extremely quiet. The frosty cold of the room has a calming effect on me. Today, without the voices, it's strangely not the least bit creepy. It's merely part of a task at a job that needs to get done. I select a transport gurney, mount the fake top into position, and pull it out of the morgue.

The emergency room is on the hospital's first floor and is a short walk from the morgue. When the architects designed the hospital in the nineteen hundreds, they had the good sense to put the morgue closest to the emergency room.

I walk through the front double doors and go to triage. "Hi, I'm looking for Edith?"

"Edith who?" the young man in blue scrubs asks.

"I don't know." I feel anxiety rush over me. "I'm with the morgue."

He frowns. "You're supposed to come in the side door."

Bless it. I knew there would be things Ricky should have told me. "I'm sorry. I'm new."

He looks side to side, then points to the end of the cubicle section. "Tell you what, let me walk you to them."

"Thanks." I move to pull the gurney down the narrow hallway and manage to strike the back of a couple of chairs. "Sorry," I say to the incoming patients who turn to see what struck their chairs. How embarrassing.

"Where's Ricky?" the young man asks.

"He's off this weekend. I'm the new weekend person."

He looks at me again and frowns. "Okay. Well, hey, my name is Jeff. I guess I'll be seeing you occasionally. I work the same shift here."

"I'm April. I appreciate you helping me."

"No worries, we're all new at one time or another in our career."

We turn down a hallway of highly polished floors. It's a beehive of activity with nurses and doctors tracking in all different directions. "We had a bit of a rush this morning. It's calmed down in admitting for now, but they're still working on several patients. A couple of car accidents."

I nod my head. "Oh."

"Edith!" Jeff hollers.

A black-haired woman with startling blue eyes pulls up and glares at Jeff. "What."

Jeff gestures with his thumb. "Did you call for transport?"

She holds a clipboard up as if in frustration. "I can't be in two places at once." She gestures for me. "Come on."

I push the transport toward her and try to keep up. We take a left down another hallway, and I'm surprised at the emergency room area's expanse. I shouldn't be. I'm in a major city, and I should have expected the vastness of the facility.

Edith looks over her shoulder. "What in the world took you

so long?"

The tone of her question shocks me. "I had to get the gurney. I came as quickly as I could."

She doesn't respond and slams into the door of a room. I follow with the gurney. As I approach the door, I'm hit with an intense sense of vertigo. If it were not for the gurney holding me up, I'd have fallen to my knees.

"You're not listening to me!" The man's voice booms through me, rattling every cell of my body and threatening to scramble my mind.

I struggle to shake off the initial shock and see a familiar face at the center of the room. Jane beckons for me to come to her.

"Jane, you've got to get Mr. Coe out of here. Dr. Tomlin needs this room for the compound fracture from the second accident."

"I know. We'll hurry."

A wave of nausea strikes me as my sense of smell picks up on what can only be described as an incredible sickness in the air. A porta-potty at a music festival in August would smell like a rose compared to the terrible stench offending my nostrils. My stomach bubbles up, and I'm oh-so-thankful I didn't take an early lunch.

"April, hurry up. We need to clear Mr. Coe from the room," Jane says the moment Edith exits the room.

Jane doesn't see him, the giant man looming behind her. He towers over her by at least a foot and is a soft four hundred pounds. His eyes are bloodshot red, and his bald head is sweating profusely. Rivulets of glistening silver sweat color his peach-colored skin. He leans over her, his hands fisted, arms back, and yells, "I'm not dead! I can't be dead."

Don't look at him, April. Whatever you do, don't look at him. If he figures out I can hear him, he'll hound me to the end of the earth.

I understand. Honestly, I do. I imagine when I die, if I have not taken care of setting things right in my life, I'll be kicking and screaming, too.

The thing about it is this man wasn't involved in the car accidents Jeff reported to me. I'm not in the medical profession, but every ounce of my body is full of recoil from his odor. I honestly believe the man had some acute sickness. It's not likely this sort of thing snuck up on him and struck him down in his noticeable youth.

I try to be in the moment and yank the cover off the transport gurney, and promptly it slips from my hands and clatters on the floor. I lean over to pick it up and place it against the wall.

"Leave it. I'll help you put it on in a second. Let's get him loaded and out of here," Jane says. I notice she's squinting as if she has a headache. I feel a migraine coming on, myself.

I push the gurney next to the operating table and Jane comes to the side of the bed I'm on. We place our hands under the plastic encasing Mr. Coe.

"Take this stupid plastic off me! What are y'all doing!" The man's spirit jumps up and down, waving his fist wildly on the opposite side of the operating table.

"One, two, three," Jane says, and we pull Mr. Coe over into the stainless-steel tray of the gurney. While his spirit continues to jump up and down, his right fist slams into the surgical tool tray, and it flips and falls to the floor. Jane and I both look in the direction of the clanging tray, then cut our eyes back to the task of centering Mr. Coe in the transport.

"Please. PLEASE," he pleads. Mr. Coe places his hands together. "I've got folks I need to talk to. I can't be leaving them like this. Too many things are undone. Too many things have to be set right."

I feel my throat and chest tightening as I listen to him. I can't afford to let him see my emotions.

As Jane helps me set the false lid on top of the transport gurney, I ask her in order to appear normal to the ghost. "What happened to him?"

She hands me the transfer papers and points. "Sepsis."

"Sepsis? What's that? How do you even catch that?" Mr. Coe's ghost says.

I wasn't sure myself. "What is that?"

Jane rolls a shoulder. "For lack of a better term, just call it full-blown internal infection. She points at the gurney. That's the unfortunate smell. He's basically a big pus bag."

"What did you call me, woman?"

That's a visual I could do without, and I gag at Jane's description. "That doesn't sound good."

She shakes her head. "It's a terrible way to go. He had to be in a lot of pain."

"You bet I was in a lot of pain. But you're gonna be in a lot of pain if you don't put me back on that table and get a doctor to do his job."

"Did Ricky show you the side door?"

It seems like everybody knows about the side door except for me. "No, I don't know where it's at."

She gestures toward the door and grabs the front of the gurney, which I'm grateful for as it takes a good bit of muscle to get Mr. Coe rolling. "I'll show you where it's at. Everyone makes that mistake the first time."

We work our way down the hall. Nurses, doctors, and patients pay no mind to us and our 'empty' gurney; we're merely rolling it down the polished tile path. We pass by the turn to triage and front door entrance. From there, we take a turn to the right.

The hall narrows, and there are no rooms, only a few closets and an electrical and mechanical closet down this spur. A large, automatic double door appears on the left, and Jane pulls the gurney into a turn for me.

She points across a tiny bit of asphalt. "See those double doors on the other side?"

A matching pair of double doors like what we just came through is on the building across from us. "Yes."

"That's the first floor of Samford Hall. Take the elevator down one floor, and you'll be on the far side of the basement.

You'll be able to get back to your office down that hallway."

Now that would have been a helpful bit of information to know earlier. I'll have to tell Ricky thank you for not at least walking me through the emergency room route. "Thank you for your help."

"No worries."

"You chicks got this all messed up. You need to go back and get the doctor and tell him to work a little magic on me. Jamie Coe has more living to do. I got some folks I got to set things right with. This isn't gonna work for me."

I get it. Man, do I get it. There are a lot of things that aren't working for me in my life, too. But at least I'm still in the game. I can only imagine what Jamie is going through as he comes to grips with the fact the time on his game clock reads all zeros.

"I'm serious. I just need another chance. I didn't realize this was as serious as it was. I mean, I knew it hurt, and I should go see the doctor. It's just doctors are expensive. Plus, most of the time, they just want to give you more pills. Come on, please listen to me."

I push through the double doors on the opposite side. It takes me a second, but I realize if I turn to the left, the morgue will be on my left fifty feet down the hallway.

I'm conscious of my sneakers squeaking on the buffed floor. One wheel of the gurney squeals with the need for oil.

When I get back to the office, I'll check to see if there is some WD-40. I don't want to be wheeling the gurneys up and down the hallway while the wheels squealing draws attention. It defeats the purpose of the covert design of the transport.

The distraction is working for me until I hear Jamie start to sob. I turn my head sideways as my throat tightens, and I desperately try not to let his tears affect me.

"Lady, please. I got a boy I need to teach how to be a man. How to live right." He chokes up. The tears well in my eyes, and my nose twitches as if I'll sneeze and begins to run.

Thankfully, I'm at the morgue entrance, and I pull my keys to unlock the wooden double doors.

"He doesn't know me. His mom won't let me around. I guess I understand, but I get it now."

Pushing Mr. Coe into the transfer room, I pull the double doors closed behind me while struggling to hold back my tears. I start to swipe at my nose and realize my hand has a latex glove on it. Exhaling, I begin to enter his name into the logbook.

"Lady, listen to me. I got stuff that has to be set right. It can't be left this way. Don't you have a heart?"

The tears come like dual waterfalls, and the snot runs freely from my nose as I wheel him in. "Yes, I have got a heart." I thump my finger against my chest. "I feel every bit of your pain, and I don't even know you. But, Jamie, you're dead. And there ain't nothing I can do about it."

He leans back and stares at me. "You can hear me?"

"Yes," I say as I wipe my nose on my arm. "Loud and clear."

He smiles. "Then, I'm alive."

There will be no "win" in this conversation for me. I move to the cooler and yank on the long handle opening the cavernous freezer door of the walk-in room. Turning, I remove the false top from the gurney.

"What are you waiting for? Go get the doc. Tell him I'm still alive."

"No, Jamie. You're dead. Don't make it hard on yourself. Go ahead and pass to the other side of the veil," I say as I push him into the cooler.

"Other side of the veil? What are you talking about?"

I position Jamie close to the other two patients who've already left this side of the veil. Maybe by spending some time close to them, he'll figure it out. I know I told him all I could, and it's up to him now.

Moving across the freezer door threshold, I pull the heavy door toward me as he screams. "Hey, you can't leave me in here. I'll die."

Shaking my head as I close the thick door, I double-check to make sure the seal has set correctly. I turn out the lights and lock the double doors before making my way to the break room.

I'm in luck. The break room is empty, and I walk directly to the ladies' room. I pull my gloves off and wash my hands. I try to wipe my tears and snot from my face without destroying my minimalist makeup job.

Sure, what Jamie said is heart-wrenching. If anybody should understand wanting a second chance, it's me. Isn't that what I have been doing the whole time I've been in Atlanta?

But there is a significant difference. Jamie made his bad decisions. It wasn't like somebody made him not take care of himself or made him not have good relationships with the people in his life.

Now I'm just justifying. It's wrong of me to judge someone when I have not walked in their shoes, and I know that at the core. But the pain inside me is unbearable, and I must find some way to alleviate it.

I look at the time and see I'd typically be at lunch if things were going to schedule. Honestly, I don't think I can eat right now. Not even cookies and cream ice cream sounds good.

But I do need to get out of here. Maybe catching some fresh air would do me good.

Stepping out of the break room, I note the double doors are closer than the front entrance. Now that I know where they lead, I decide I'll go out that way and do some exploring. The distraction will take my mind off Jamie Coe.

The double doors swing open automatically. As I come across the rubber mat, I see a familiar face outside the ER. Jane is sitting on a five-gallon bucket turned upside down. Her legs are hooked at the knees, and her right foot is bouncing nervously as she takes a drag on a cigarette. She blows a gray-blue ribbon of smoke into the air.

Making my way across the pavement, I ask her, "Is this a private moment?"

She points to an empty plastic grocery carrier turned up-side down. I pull it closer and sit next to her.

"I thought you were off today."

She pulls the cigarette from her lips and holds it propped a few inches from her face. "Was supposed to be. If I were smart, I would have been."

I don't know what to say to that. We stare at each other.

She flips her hand holding the cigarette. "A couple of the other nurses called in sick. Staffing asked me if I could cover, and here I am."

"Oh."

She shakes her body side to side as she says sarcastically, "Just call Jane. She'll cover. She doesn't have a life. All she does is work and save money."

"I'm sorry. I'm sure they appreciate it."

She looks at me and frowns. "I doubt it." She takes a drag on her cigarette and blows the smoke leisurely into the air. She holds it out to me in an offer for me to take a puff.

"No, thanks, I can't."

"Smart girl. I wish I'd never started. I don't need them very often anymore. But I carry a pack for backup in case my nerves get shot."

"I'd carry a pint of ice cream if it would keep in my purse," I offer.

She glares at me and then bursts into laughter. "Girl, I would too. Lord knows it would taste better than this stupid cigarette."

"But you couldn't blow the cool smoke trail into the air."

"That's true."

We sit in companionable silence—two girls with a rough day that's not even half done.

"You know it's okay to tell people you don't want to cover for somebody else. You have a right to have a weekend off," I say.

She studies me for a moment, then exhales. "The work

keeps my mind off the fact that all I do is work."

In a strange, twisted way, that makes all the sense in the world to me. "What would you rather be doing?"

"I don't know. But there has to be more to life than just working."

I have my doubts some days. As I run my life through my mind, except for the last couple of months which have in no way been fun, it seems like all I have been doing is a lot of work too.

There was the year in college where I was a party queen. Before that, in middle school and high school, I worked my tail off to earn excellent grades to get into college. After a few semesters of low cumulative scores at Alabama, I worked extremely hard for six years to make the grade while working a part-time job.

"You're good at your job." What I have seen of her so far, I believe that to be true.

She favors me with a wan smile. "Thanks."

I draw a deep breath and scoot my grocery carton back far enough to lean against the brick wall. I look up at the sky. I see it's a cloudless day, but the buildings on either side are so tall we are in complete shade. It's as if we're concealed from the entire world.

I can't help myself, and I ask, "Are you upset because Ricky didn't ask you to do something this weekend?"

She scrunches up her face as she looks at me. "I hadn't even thought about that little turkey. But yeah, I suppose if homeboy would quit looking and start asking, it would be a nice diversion to have something to do on my days off. At least then I could tell the staffing director I already have plans and not feel like I'm lying to them."

I get fidgety and am about to go to the cafeteria and see if I can work up an appetite. Before I do, Jane pulls out another cigarette and lights it.

"Can I tell you something, and you not share it with anybody else?"

I shrug my shoulders. "I suppose."

"This job will kill me. It's not what I thought it would be when I was going through nursing school." She pauses and thins her lips. "That's not true. The medical part is. And I enjoy it, and to your point, I feel I'm good at it. But like what just happened with Mr. Coe. April, I'm afraid it's gonna kill me."

A lot of folks do have a tough time with death. If Jane is one of them, it is unfortunate she spent her time and money earning an education in the nursing field. True fact, people don't come to the hospital because they're well. If they're at the hospital, often they're at risk of being someone who might die.

"Why do you say that?"

"You know people ought to just take better care of themselves," she says.

I feel slightly self-conscious about the extra fifteen pounds I'm carrying. "I won't disagree with that."

She points in the morgue's general direction. "Do you know how many Mr. Coes we see in a week?"

"I haven't a clue."

"Too many to count, that's how many. Same sad story. He's a man who should be in the prime of his life and pushes away his family and friends and then sets out to destroy his body until his body says, 'Screw you, Bud, I'm out.'" She shakes her head. "It's a sorry state of affairs. "

"Is there something else you can do as a nurse? Maybe some sort of research or a lab technician?"

"Why?"

"If being around death bothers you. You said you were saving money. Maybe when you get to the point you can afford to, just go ahead and take the time you need to retrain." I shrug. "I assume if you're a nurse, you'll have to deal with people dying regularly. But we all deal with it, Jane. Medical professionals more, but the rest of us are forced to face it, too."

Jane drops her cigarette and crushes it under her sneaker.

She leans forward with her head propped on her hands. "It's not the death part. April."

I'm surprised. "Then what is it?"

"I can hear them." She lifts her head, her eyes narrow slits now. "I can hear them after they pass. They're crying or angry. But they're always asking for more time."

My face goes through ten different contortions in three seconds as I realize Jane has some psychic ability level. I try to put on a calm, understanding expression.

I think I fail.

"You probably think I'm crazy, girl. Maybe I am." She exhales. "Probably time to use that medical insurance I never use and go see a counselor." She puts her finger to her temple and makes a whirly motion. "Maybe they can figure out what's all screwed up in here because nobody hears voices from dead people. Leastways not anybody sane."

I consider telling Jane she most definitely did hear Jamie Coe talking. And also share with her, I not only heard him but saw the massive man. But as much as I'd like to help her, I'm not ready to share that sort of personal information with her even though she's shared it with me.

I'm not sure if that makes me a terrible person or not. But presently, that's my decision.

She gestures toward the emergency room doors. "I have probably taken too long of a break. I'll catch up with you later, okay."

"Yeah, sure. I'll see you around, Jane."

Chapter 17

I take the elevator to the cafeteria to see if I can find something that sparks my appetite. I go through the line looking at my options. While the cafeteria has a diverse selection I'd eagerly eat on an average day, with Jamie Coe on my mind, I'm not hungry.

I opt for an ice cream sandwich instead of real food and eat half of it by myself at a table in the far corner. Jamie's messed my head up bad.

Not because his spirit talked to me or that he was able to force his way so quickly through my partition. I have dealt with hostile spirits before. In fact, on a recent trip to Pensacola, I was roughed up by a ghost one night. Not saying Jamie's violent. Because he doesn't give me any indication to think he would hurt me.

What has my mind messed up is his inability to come to grips with "game over." I don't know why, but until this moment, I don't believe I ever considered what it takes for a spirit to come to peace with the fact they're dead. I have known for a long time when someone dies, they don't just go dark and disappear into the nothingness with no conscious thoughts and only blackness around them.

No, their spirits move on. Once energy—always energy—constantly changing—but can never be destroyed. At least that's what Nana told me.

I don't think Jamie is going to move across of his own volition. And that makes me sad for him because there is nothing left for him on this side of the veil. Staying can only be a frustrating proposition. One that could turn him mean and vengeful with time.

I don't know him, but I wouldn't wish that curse on anybody. I really do wish there were some way I could help him, but I'm at a loss.

The morgue cell phone rings, startling me back to the present. "Metro Morgue, April speaking."

"Hi, this is Billy Wright with Atkins Funeral Home. I wanted to let you know I'll be at your location in five minutes to pick up Ms. Schultz."

"Sure. I'll meet you at the morgue in a few minutes, Billy. I'm just finishing lunch."

"Thank you."

The half of the ice cream sandwich I didn't eat has melted onto the foil, and I must be careful how I lift it up so as not to spill it. I drop it off at the garbage on the way out.

Taking the elevator down to the basement, my mind is preoccupied with one thought. Please let Jamie have already crossed the veil. The last thing I want to do is release Ms. Schultz to Billy, with Jamie screaming at me about me needing to find him a doctor. I have built the partitions in my mind as sturdy as possible. Still, Jamie's energy level is too new and too powerful for anyone to block him. He comes like a hurricane wave forcing its way over the seawalls. That's why Jane, who I assume has a lower level of psychic ability, heard him. He's a powerful, supernatural force.

As I walk the hallway, I see a tall, thin man standing by the morgue with a gurney. The gurney has a bright red crushed velvet cover on it that reads Atkins Funeral Home.

With his lean build, wireframe glasses, and large Adam's apple, Billy reminds me of Ichabod Crane from Sleepy Hollow. Sort of apropos given all the paranormal going on in the morgue right now.

"Hi, Billy, sorry to keep you waiting," I say as I pull out my keys.

"I actually just arrived. You're new."

I look over my shoulder as I open the door. "Yes, my name is April. I'll be working the weekend shift."

"Okay. Well nice to meet you."

I locate Ms. Shultz's entry in the logbook, sign, and point for Billy to sign, too. He does, and I turn to open the cooler door.

Before I touch the door, I hear Jamie. "Where did you go?"

I'm not doing this with Jamie. I pull open the massive door and walk purposefully to the two smaller patients and check their tags. Finding Ms. Shultz, I pull her gurney toward the door.

"Don't ignore me. I know you can hear me."

"So, where is Atkins Funeral Home?" I ask.

Billy smiles. "Adamsville. It's out on the west side of town."

No, I really don't care. And I have no idea where Adamsville is. I'm just asking so Jamie might believe I can't hear him any longer.

I offer to help Billy pull Ms. Shultz onto his gurney, but he does it in one quick motion. She must be a featherweight because he didn't even look like he exerted himself.

Billy puts the fake cover back on his gurney and then the bright funeral home cover over it. I open the double doors for him, and he wheels Ms. Shultz out.

"Until next time," he says cheerfully.

I lift a hand in salutation. "Have a great day."

As I turn to lock the transfer room's door, Jamie screams at me again. I close the door and walk toward the office. Checking my phone on the way back, I see it's only two o'clock. There are five more hours I'll have to avoid Jamie Coe.

Chapter 18

In a show of mental discipline, I force my attention back to my studies. If I don't pass the bar exam on the first try next month, I'll be stuck dealing with more men like Jamie Coe, according to Jane, or I'll have to go home in defeat.

My phone rings; that's a welcome distraction. When I see who's calling, I groan. "I'm such a sucky friend."

It's my friend Martin Culp from law school. Understand, Martin is an incredible friend, and I love talking to him. The problem is, the last few times it's been him calling me, not me calling him. A testimony to how much better of a friend he is to me than I am to him.

"Hey, buddy, have you worked up any trade deals lately?" I ask.

"Hi." Martin draws the two-letter word out for a few syllables. I can tell he's hesitating.

"Cat got your tongue?"

"Well yeah, I was calling to give you the cool news. One of your schoolmates has been assigned to the task force reworking the trade deal with a major country. Kind of a big deal."

"Get out of town."

"Don't go over the top. I'm just one of the lackeys on the payroll to write what is negotiated, but pretty cool. Right?"

"Way cool! Congratulations. You didn't take long to make

your mark."

"Just blind luck. Remember when I worked with representative Thompson two summers ago during my first internship."

I don't remember that. "Sure."

"He's been using my template ever since. When the trade negotiations started with Senator Larson in charge, Thompson put a bug in his ear that I was a hot commodity. Then I got the assignment."

My curiosity gets the best of me, plus I know Martin can't keep a secret. "Who's the big-time country."

"I could tell you, but then I'd have to kill you."

I shake my head. Martin picked the saying up from his daddy, a *Top Gun* fan, and he's used it as long as I have known him. "No. Seriously, give me a hint. Don't tell me. I just want a hint."

"Well, I guess a clue wouldn't hurt. It's an Asian country."

I have a reasonably clear idea of which country, but I know I can get it out of Martin. "That's no help. I mean, I don't even know any Asian countries except Australia."

Martin laughs. "You really should have taken at least one geography course. Australia is not Asian."

If he could see me, he would know I'm toying with him since I'm grinning from ear to ear. "What, I know it's close to over there, and it starts with an A."

"That doesn't even make sense, Snow."

"Then give me something useful. At least give me the first letter of the country's name."

Martin hesitates again and then, all serious-like he says, "C."

"Oh, wow. Cambodia, that's awesome." It's been all over the news. A team of senators is tasked with rewriting the trade deal with China.

"I guess that's close enough. What's going on in your life? Have you made partner yet?"

"No, not quite yet. It might be a little while." I struggle with whether I should tell him the truth. Martin is a good friend, and he wouldn't think any less of me, but I can't bring myself to share.

"Yeah, but I know you're enjoying those paychecks. A few years from now, I might wish I had been smart like you and taken the money instead."

"I'm sure you'll do quite fine right where you're at, Martin. Besides, you always wanted to work in politics. You better do it while you're young before you have any responsibilities."

"Are you okay?"

Bless it, I knew I was talking too much. "Sure, why do you ask?"

"You just sound sort of forlorn or unhappy. You are happy, aren't you?"

"Happy as a pig in mud. I am tired, though. You know the work schedule is pretty brutal."

"Tell me about it. They expect us to be machines with no need to eat, sleep, or pee. I'm easily working seventy hours a week. Like you say, besides learning and working right now, I don't have much going on."

I almost ask him if he's dating anyone, but I learned my mistake from an earlier conversation when I asked him. Martin's former girlfriend, Penny, was murdered by a serial killer a few months back. Of course, Martin's not seeing anybody yet. He's still recovering.

"Don't let them work you to death. I'd hate to have to come up there and knock some heads," I say.

He laughs. "I miss you, Snow."

"Back at you, buddy."

"Oh, I almost forgot. I hope you don't mind, but I did mention you to Senator Larson. He's impressed with your résumé, as he should be. You need to know you have an open invitation if you ever decide you want to come up to DC and practice on the Hill."

"I don't think the swamp is ready for me, Martin."

He laughs again. "I disagree with you. We could use another

alpha gator in the swamp."

"Okay, now you're just silly."

"Well, like I said, it's an open invitation. I can think of at least one junior attorney who would be happy to see you in town."

"Thank you, Martin. Thank you for the call; it's brightened my day."

"Always happy to be of service. Later, Snow."

"Later, Martin." I hang up, but the glow from the conversation stays with me. I think about the hundreds of meals and thousands of beers Martin and I shared together over our three years in law school. It seems odd now we're not directly in each other's lives. Thankfully, one of us is a good friend.

Do better, April.

The conversation with him seems to help me focus on the material I'm trying to study. Case law is a topic that some days is exciting to me. Other days, I'm not focused on it and have a challenging time comprehending the finer points of the case. It's not a difficulty of the topic issue. It's an April paying attention issue.

Now I'm in the zone. My mind is particularly sticky as I'm reading over the cases. I should call Martin before all my study sessions.

Chapter 19

"That looks like a fascinating book."

I look up to see Marjorie standing in the doorway. "Hi." I look down at my phone.

"Yep, time flies when you're having fun," Marjorie says as she strolls into the office.

She's right. It's 6:55 p.m., and my shift is over. I gather up my books.

"Anything interesting happen today?"

I drop one of my books. "Nope. All quiet," I say as I pick it up.

"That's just the way you want it in the morgue. Quiet."

If she only knew. "You've got Ms. Whitaker and Mr. Coe left in the morgue."

She wrinkles her nose. "Ms. Whitaker is still here?"

"Yes, her funeral home called a couple hours ago and said they wouldn't be here until around ten."

Marjorie sits down in the chair and puts her feet on the desk. "Good. That means I get at least three hours of sleep. I did a little too much partying at the pool today."

"Okay, I'll see you in the morning," I say, opening the office door.

"Good night."

Walking to the parking deck, I'm assessing the day in my mind and realize this is doable. Sure, Mr. Coe threw me for a loop. But I really don't expect spirits of his strength to be a common occurrence. And even if they are, I feel the more I'm exposed to them, the better I'll get at controlling their power surge. Like my healing abilities that I didn't even know I had until a few weeks ago, and now little by little, I'm getting better control over them.

There is a significant difference between hearing and seeing ghosts and helping someone by giving them a little healing juice. If you heal someone, at least you know you did some good. I can't help but think my conversation with Jamie Coe only left his spirit more frustrated. I wish I knew how to help him.

I know it's not like he deserves anyone to do anything for him. In all fairness, it sounds like he was a complete lowlife. His situation, in my experience, is not unusual. I have seen folks who don't realize they're wasting their time and relationship clout until they no longer have them available.

My brother Chase has a significant rock-and-roll collection. This includes music from the big hair bands. It reminds me of one of the songs by a group called Cinderella he plays whenever he is melancholy. The song is called "Don't Know What You Got Till It's Gone." Isn't that the truth of things?

When I unlock my car, the heat rolls out of it, and I wait a second before I try to get in. I'm so ready for fall to get here.

I get in and pull out of the parking deck. Approaching the state highway that will take me to my apartment, my cell phone rings.

"Hello?"

"April, this is Shane."

As if I wouldn't know. "Hey, what's up?"

"I was about to ask you the same thing. Do you think you might be free tonight?"

My stomach takes flight, and I begin to grin like a loon. "Yeah, sure. What do you have in me?" My skin flashes hot. "Mind."

"I have got a huge favor to ask. I called agencies all over

Atlanta today. No one has a twenty-four-hour caregiver available to cover for me next week when I'm in Cincinnati. I'd cancel, but this training is only offered twice a year. If I don't get certified now, Dr. Hamlin will have to bump me from the team."

So many details to unpack at one time, not to mention my disappointment this isn't a date call. Plus, I'm sweating from my Freudian slip, which seems to have flown harmlessly past Shane's comprehension. "Okay."

"I know it's a huge imposition, and I have no right to ask it, and I absolutely wouldn't if I were not desperate. But, April, is there any way you could stay with Pop next week?"

It's weird. Last night I was trying to make this arrangement work in my head, and it seemed like a promising idea. But now that Shane is the one presenting it to me, it makes absolutely no sense. "But I have an eight-hour shift Tuesday and Thursday."

"I have got that covered—Connie McPherson. She lives up the street and was a good friend of my grandmother's. She can come and keep Pop company Tuesday and Thursday. I just need you to stay with him for the rest of the time. I'll be back Friday night."

My head is swimming, and I'm having difficulty processing everything.

"April, I know that'll cut into your interviewing time, and like I said, I promise you I wouldn't ask if I wasn't just totally up against the wall here. Connie can only watch him those two days. She has a mother in Stockbridge she has to check in on and make sure she takes her medications." He stops, catches his breath. "It's just I have never known him to take to someone the way he's taken to you. I could be at ease if you were with him next week. I'd pay you. His caregivers make good money."

My body tenses. "I'm not gonna take your money, Shane. I'll do it, but as a favor, like you've done for me."

"Thank you." He exhales. "You're a lifesaver."

"So, what was this about tonight?"

"I thought you could come up, and we can go over his medication and some of the routines he has. It'll make it easier on you once you're alone with him."

"When do you leave?"

"Monday morning."

Which means I either do it tonight or tomorrow night. I guess there is no time like the present. "Okay. I need to swing by my apartment first and get some clothes. I'd rather just leave straight from the lake home for work in the morning."

"Okay. That's a good idea. I'll get the spare guest room set up."

"I'll see you in a little while."

"Thank you again, April. See you in a bit."

For the life of me, I can't figure out what's wrong with me. Last night, this is precisely what I wanted. Instead of asking and explaining the situation to Shane, he's made it like I'm doing him a favor. This is a great trial run. Assuming it works out well for John Michael and me over the week by ourselves.

In that case, it'll be that much easier to transition into living with him until I pass the bar exam. Everybody wins in that situation.

So why am I feeling uneasy?

Chapter 20

Pulling into the driveway of John Michael's lake home, I'm surprised to see Shane waiting in the driveway. I park my car and get out. "What's up?"

He comes within inches of me. "I just need to warn you before you come in. Pop is having a manic episode."

Odd. "Is he normally bipolar?"

Shane shrugs. "Before I told him you were staying with him next week, he's never been. But he's like a three-year-old after scarfing a family-sized bag of Skittles for the last hour. He's darn near talked me to death."

I can't help but laugh. "He's probably just happy to have some company for the week."

"He's never acted this way for me," Shane grumbles.

"It's the newness. It'll wear off." I go to the back of my car and pop the hatch.

"Let me get that for you."

I start to say no and then think, why not milk this for all it's worth and let him get my bag. I shut the hatch and follow him to the front door.

"I didn't have time to cook, so I hope you don't mind. I picked up some fried chicken."

"I wasn't expecting dinner, so that's a bonus, Shane."

We step into the house, and John Michael greets me a few

feet in. "We're going to have a fun time this week, April."

Shane's right. He's so animated it reminds me of staring into a light fixture that's too bright. "I hope so."

"You will if you mind your manners, Pop," Shane says as he turns to the right, going down the small hallway I didn't investigate yesterday.

John Michael puts his hand to the side of his face and looks at me. "He's a stick in the mud."

I roll my eyes at him and then follow Shane down the hallway.

"I had to take my stuff out of here, but I think I have got it picked up where it's not a total embarrassment."

He's nervous. It's cute. "I'm sure it'll be fine." Stepping into the room, I feel like I have tripped through a time portal and fell into a Sears catalog bedroom from circa 1990.

Shane looks around and appears self-conscious. "The decor is a little dated, but I changed out the mattress just last year. It's really comfortable."

A vision of Shane in nothing but his boxers lying on the bed pushes into my mind. I feel my neck blush.

Shane shifts on his feet uneasily. "I'll stay in the den tonight. I'm hoping you can stay tomorrow night too. My flight leaves at seven in the morning Monday."

I nod my head and walk over to the bed to start unpacking my bag. Shane gestures toward the door. "I'll let you be while you unpack. When you're ready, come on out, and we'll have dinner. After that, I'll show you the medications he's on."

Exciting stuff. "Okay."

Shane stops in the doorway and looks back at me. "I'm sorry. I know this is just the weirdest thing in the world. But I really appreciate it."

"It's not weird, and I'm glad you asked since you needed help." That's the truth, too.

He smiles and taps the doorway. Then I'm alone.

Taking a second, I scan my new surroundings. More accurate, my new home for the week. If everything works out, my new home until I'm successfully employed at an Atlanta firm.

It reminds me of a little boy's room. There are no specific items to prompt that perception in my mind, no army men, cowboys or Indians, or pinup model posters. It's just a general feeling I get. I also take note there is no paranormal energy in the room.

I can't say the same for the room across the hallway. I felt the prickle on the back of my neck as I walked by it. The door is pulled shut. Of course, my curiosity is spinning. I want to know what's inside the room and why the door needs to be closed.

My curiosity can wait. There will be plenty of time next week to explore what lies behind the door. And since there is paranormal energy, if I were smart, which often lately I can't claim, I'd leave well enough alone. An intelligent girl would leave the door shut.

The drawers of the dresser beside the bed are empty. Either Shane doesn't use this room often, or he went through a lot of trouble to take all his clothes out. Sweet.

I unpack my bag, storing my clothes in the dresser. When I get to my makeup case, I poke my head out of the bedroom door and am pleased to see a small bathroom to my right. This is an excellent layout except for the weird room across the hall.

I stow my makeup case in the bathroom, wash my hands, and head toward the kitchen.

John Michael is sitting at the dinette table with a half tumbler of bourbon. "I thought I was going to have to send the Marines after you," he says.

I favor him with a smile and turn to Shane. "Besides fried chicken, what do you have?"

He unpacks the large family-sized container. "Green beans, mashed potatoes and gravy, and biscuits."

"Yes, yes, and yes," I say.

"I want a thigh," John Michael says. "I'm a thigh man."

I don't know why that tickles me, but I conceal my laugh

again. I'm afraid of what will happen if I start to encourage John Michael by laughing.

After dinner, we watch another half episode of *The Walking Dead*. When John Michael falls asleep, Shane helps him to bed.

Returning from the master bedroom, Shane gestures for me to come to the kitchen. "If you have a minute, I'd like to go over his medications with you."

"Sure." I get up from the sofa and go to him.

"I have got it all listed out here on this notebook." Shane flips open a three-ring binder and points at a laminated sheet.

"OCD much?" I ask.

"It's been such a revolving door with caregivers, it's easier to write the directions down and then make sure they don't fall apart with time."

I look at the list and arch my eyebrows. "My gosh. No wonder the man doesn't eat. You're filling his stomach up on chemicals."

Shane's lips thin. "It's the cancer. Most of this is a regiment to try and slow the spread."

"Is it working?" The question blurts out before I realize I was going to ask it. I can't believe I'm so insensitive.

"I'm not an oncologist, so I don't know. Honestly, though, I don't feel like it is."

"Fair." I point at the instructions. "It'll be easier for me to memorize them if you show me the actual containers."

Shane and I spend thirty minutes reviewing the details of each medication. To help me remember them, I ask him to explain what each one is supposed to do. It seems like many of them are supposed to do the same thing and counteract one another in a few cases. I'm not sure if John Michael is getting healthier, but somebody should be able to send their kids through college with all these prescriptions.

I look at my phone when we finish going through the last item. It's eleven o'clock. "I better get to bed."

"Okay, do you want me to leave the hall light on for you?"

"Why?"

"I just thought you might want it, so you don't get scared if you wake up."

"No, but I could really use a nightlight if you have one."

"Maybe we have one—"

I roll my eyes. "I'm kidding, Shane." I walk down the hall. "Good night."

"Good night, April."

Stripping down to my panties, I pull a T-shirt on and get into bed. I have never been the biggest fan of strange beds. Still, Shane is correct. The mattress is to die for.

Throwing back the covers, I get back out of bed. Not because I'm scared, but I'm feeling modest. I lock my bedroom door and return to bed.

Bless it. I almost forget to set my alarm. Grabbing my phone, I set the alarm for five a.m. Geez, that seems early. But I'll need a shower, and it's a forty-five-minute drive to work from here.

I pull the covers up. They feel nice and cool against my skin.

I'm dreaming, or I feel like I am. I'm in a swamp, and I'm trying to avoid the gators. I'm wading through murky, waist-deep water.

Thanks for putting it in my head, Martin.

There is a ten-foot gator tracking a few feet behind me. I move my feet as quickly as possible up and down on the mucky floor of the swamp. Looking over my shoulder, I see the gator, and it's still the same distance behind me.

I come to a stop. My hair is stuck, and something is pulling on it. Turning, I see a clump of my hair is twisted in a briar bush. The thorns hold my hair tightly, and I can't pull free.

My heart races as the gator, sensing its opportunity, swings its thick tail side to side, propelling its open maw toward me.

I yank my hair, but it will not come loose. Twisting the briar branch, I try to break it off, but it only bends. The more I struggle, the tighter its grip on my hair.

I gasp for air as my eyes pop open. The room is dimly lit from the silver moon shining between the blind slats. I suck my breath in as I notice a young girl near my pillow, holding my hair in her hand.

Her hair is light, silver in the moonlight. It's difficult to tell, but I feel she might be ten years old or a little older.

I try to remain still and not look at the young girl to the best of my ability. My body trembles, and she cuts her sparkling green eyes toward my face.

I'm frightened, and I pull away. When I do, she drops my hair and disappears through the door.

My curiosity screams for me to follow her. My common sense tells me to stay put, and I quickly vote for the latter. Still, I don't fall back asleep. It's just a little too freaky for me to wake up and have a ghost examining me that closely.

Chapter 21

Marjorie's asleep when I come in. I tap her foot. Her eyes open, and I say, "Good morning, sunshine."

She drops her feet from the desk and yawns. "Boring night. You've got a clean house except for Mr. Coe."

I totally forgot about Mr. Coe. My spirits sink. "Any word on when they're picking him up?"

"Funny you should ask. I got a call from the county social worker about an hour ago. No one's claiming him."

"He didn't have any family?"

Marjorie gathers her purse and puts its strap on her shoulder. "I think he had a family. They just don't want him."

Ouch. Harsh.

"I'll see you tonight. Have a good shift."

"Thanks," I say.

I put in a full three hours of studying without any interruptions. In some ways, it's better to review the textbooks at the morgue office than at the library. At the library, people are moving around. I have such an intense natural curiosity, I tend to be people-watching when I should be studying. Plus, there is nothing in the small office to allow me to daydream. It is merely plain gray walls, one desk, one chair, and the morgue phone on the desk that's not ringing. Not a lot to inspire the imagination.

I put a bookmark in my textbook and sit back for a second. I could stand a walk just to break the monotony, but I have something else on my mind.

It's none of my business, and I have a suspicion he didn't do anything in his life to earn it. Still, it's been bugging me ever since I thought about the difference between talking to ghosts and helping someone with my healing skills. There must be a way my communication-with-the-dead ability can help someone. I obviously just have not figured it out yet.

If there was a time to try, it would be now. If Mr. Coe hasn't gone through the veil yet, I could see what he wants. Obviously, I couldn't help him with his requests yesterday. He was asking for the doctors to make him alive again. And I explained that to him. But maybe I can do something to put his mind at ease and allow him to let go of this world.

Yeah, I really don't want to do this. The whole talking-to-the-dead thing will always give me the heebie-jeebies. Live people shouldn't talk to dead people. If it's not a law, it should be.

Leaning back, I consider taking a nap instead, like Marjorie did with her feet on the desk. I'm not tired, but I decide to try it. Putting my feet on the desk, I try to get comfortable. It's not very comfortable, and it kinda hurts my tailbone.

I slap my feet back down on the floor. All right, I'm so fidgety I'm driving myself nuts.

Exhaling loudly, I decide I don't have much to lose. Well, besides my sanity. I pick up the keys and make my way toward the morgue.

I have not even unlocked the double doors, and I feel Mr. Coe's energy. He hasn't left. If anything, his power has grown.

I close the double doors behind me and open the freezer door. Jamie's arms are crossed, and he has light frost on his eyebrows. "You again," he says.

"You're still here?"

"Where should I be?" he asks.

"The burial service is coming to get you. It would probably

be best if you leave before then."

"I told you I have things that need to be fixed first," he snarls.

"How can I help?" I ask.

"Oh, now you care."

I point toward the door. "I can always leave."

He raises a hand. "No, please don't. I'm sorry. This is all sort of weird."

"Jamie, understand what's weird is you have not passed over to the other side. If you'd done that, you wouldn't even care anymore."

He drops his chin to his chest and shakes it. "You know, that really sounds good. But I have got a boy. I don't really know him, but I want him to know I care about him. He needs to know I thought about him a lot."

I lower my voice. "Jamie, I understand that. But it's done. None of us get to finish life exactly how we want to. I'm sure you did the best you could do, and now it's time to leave."

"No!" His energy buffets me. "If I can just let him know his dad cares, it would make all the difference in the world. I mean, if I had just known … if he had just told me, it might have made a difference in my life."

I get it now. I'm looking at a man who didn't know the face of his father, and as much as he hated that aspect of his life, he just doomed his own son to the same circumstance. He gifted the curse of his generation to his son's and grandson's relationship. I can understand where that failure is something he would seek to correct if there were any way possible.

"Tell me how to help."

"I have been thinking. I can't go to him. And even if I could, it's not right to scare a seven-year-old by appearing when I'm dead."

"That's pretty sound logic," I agree.

He gives me the stink eye. "No reason to be smart-alecky about it."

"Sorry."

"I thought if maybe I wrote a letter to him. You know something that he could pull out whenever he's sad and read how his daddy loves him."

I let his comment hang in the air. I don't want to be the one to tell him I think that's an awful idea.

"What do you think?"

You know it doesn't matter; his goal isn't my goal. My goal is to help him pass to the other side of the veil. "If I help you, will you promise to be at peace and move on to the other side?"

"There is nothing here for me." He waves his arm. "I'll want to go after I know he understands how I feel about him."

"I'll help you, but I don't know how we do this. I can deliver a letter for you, but if you don't write it—it won't be in your handwriting."

"I have been thinking about that, too. What if you said I had the letter in my pocket, and when I came in, it got bloody, and so you wrote it down on a card to give to him."

"But you died of sepsis. There wasn't any blood."

Jamie rolls his eyes again. "He's seven years old. He doesn't know there wasn't any blood."

Seems like we're defeating the purpose if we're going to lie to him to make this happen, but again, my goal is to get Jamie to the other side of the veil. Anything else will just be a cherry on top.

"Fine." I pull out my phone. "Tell me what you want to say to your son, and I'll dictate it into my phone. Later, I'll transcribe it to a card for you."

Mr. Coe left before the end of my shift. The social workers picked him up a little less than an hour after giving me the long message he wants me to deliver to his son.

Unfortunately, there was a death in the ER and one up in the East Tower's ICU. When Marjorie came, I told her about the two new patients and walked to the parking deck.

As I get in the car, I call Shane. "Hey, what are you doing?"

"Trying to get packed."

"Do you like spaghetti?"

"There are people in the world who don't like it?"

"There is always a first for everything."

"Are you offering?"

I get a tingle just below my navel. "I'm always offering."

He gives a husky laugh that intensifies my tingle. "Yes, I'd love some, please. That actually works out great since I'm still putting together everything I need to take on the trip."

"Good. I'll be there in the hour."

No, initially, it wasn't my plan to cook spaghetti. But Shane is leaving in the morning, and I need to run into the grocery store to get a card for Jamie's message to his son. I figure I might as well kill two good deeds with one grocery store run.

Chapter 22

When I get to John Michael's lake house, I make a beeline for the kitchen. Shane comes in and offers to help, but I quickly shoo him out. I have got this. My brother Dusty has shown me his ultra-easy mushroom marinara, and I'm a girl on a mission.

It's exhilarating, the idea of cooking dinner for two guys I really like. I search through the cupboards and come up with the two stockpots I'll need—one with a Teflon bottom and one to boil the noodles.

I feel light and alive as I pour the olive oil in the silver pot and throw a tablespoon of garlic in it to sauté. As the garlic releases its fragrance, I understand.

Mama is always beautiful when cooking her lasagna because it makes her feel like I feel right now. Doing something special for people you love? I swear I feel like I'm shining as bright as a star.

I struggle a little further down the recipe. I add the ingredients as written, dropping in a handful of onions I diced and three handfuls of sliced mushrooms.

Bless it, Dusty. Why can't you use measuring cups like everybody else? I can't decide how much larger his hands are than mine.

Once the mushrooms and onions have been sautéed with

the garlic, I add the tomato sauce and cans of diced tomatoes. Then the Italian seasoning. I forget if it was four or five table-spoons to add, but more is better.

As the red concoction bubbles, it smells exactly right, and my mouth salivates. These guys are going to be so surprised. They're in for a special treat. I'm so proud of myself I can hardly stand it.

The water for the noodles in the black Teflon pot begins to steam lightly as I place the frozen garlic toast into the oven. I have it timed out where everything will be ready together in fifteen minutes.

"Guys! Dinner will be ready in ten."

The water starts to boil, and I dump the noodles while grabbing a colander placing it in the sink. Yep, my timing is perfect.

I go to give the bubbly marinara sauce a quick stir. My wooden spoon sticks at the bottom. I push harder, and as the sauce stuck to the bottom of the pan becomes more difficult to scrape away, I realize the error of my ways. In horror, I look to my right and see the violent bubbling of the water with the noodles in the Teflon pot.

"Oh, April." I scrape fiercely at the marinara stockpot, try-ing to break free all the gooey sauce sticking to the bottom. I tell myself it's not a lost cause, even though I smell a burnt toast scent coming out of the stockpot.

As a last-ditch effort, I turn the burner off and push the marinara to the side. I continue to scrape vigorously.

When the timer goes off, I give up on the marinara and nearly burn my hands on the noodle pot when I don't grab potholders first. Shane enters the kitchen, and I catch the col-ander sideways, almost losing the noodles down the drain.

Shane's brow creases. "Smells good." It sounds more like a question than a compliment.

"Thanks," I say as I pull the bread out. John Michael wan-ders in with his tumbler of bourbon. "Something smells inter-esting."

I don't think I could feel any warmer, but my entire body has a heat flash of embarrassment, and I break into a sweat. Interesting is not what I was trying to accomplish tonight.

"Grab your bowls. You want to get your noodles before they get sticky."

"I'll get your bowl, Pop."

John Michael bumps Shane at the cupboard. "I'm perfectly capable of fixing a bowl of spaghetti for myself, son." John Michael hands me a bowl, too. "Ladies first."

I don't blame him a bit. The way it smells, I'd want him to try it before I risked my health on it if he had cooked it for me.

We fix our bowls and sit down at the dinette table. I can't help but notice three substantial sunflowers in the center, blocking my view of Shane sitting across from me. "Where did these beautiful sunflowers come from?"

"Connie brought them over this morning," John Michael says.

"Connie, the lady who will stay with you Tuesday and Thursday?"

Shane gestures with his hand. "She lives at the start of the cul-de-sac."

"She brought the sunflowers for Lulu. She knows how much she loves them," John Michael says.

Shane looks down and shakes his head as he twirls the spaghetti noodles on his fork. I want to find out more about Lulu, but I can tell by Shane's reaction that it'll be better to ask John Michael when Shane is gone on his trip.

I'm surprised when John Michael continues. "Connie's husband, Bob, served in Vietnam, too. He was a pilot."

"Were you in Vietnam, John Michael?"

He brightens as his eyes narrow. "Yes, ma'am, recon."

"Pop was one of the crazy ones. What was it they called you, Pop?"

He grins. "Tunnel rat. Whenever we would find a Viet Cong tunnel, I was the one who went in with a flashlight and a handgun to clear it out for our platoon."

I pause and study John Michael. Sometimes when I meet someone older, I can be shocked to find out what they did in their younger life. I never would have thought of John Michael as a tip-of-the-spear type warrior, but now, as he tells me about it, I see a hard edge to him that makes it plausible.

I put a bite of spaghetti in my mouth and hold it. I should have swallowed it as quickly as possible. The burnt aroma is akin to someone having stuck a cigar in the pot of marinara.

I look to both men. Shane is munching slowly on garlic toast while John Michael attacks his spaghetti sauce.

"When I got back home in '72, after my tour of duty, I took a job on the line at the Ford factory. My daddy had already worked there for twenty-plus years, and it was easy to get a job then. Paid surprisingly good money, too."

I give up on the spaghetti and, like Shane, begin munching on the garlic toast. "And your wife?"

"Angie and I had met through friends in high school. When I came back and was working at Ford, I stopped to get gas one day on the way home. Lo and behold at the pump next to me, there she was pumping gas into her little VW Beetle. I hadn't seen her in six years. She'd gone on and got her degree and had just started teaching." He smiles, and his stare looks far away as if he were back in 1972. "It was like looking at the most beautiful sunset you've ever seen, except it's a person. She just glowed, and I knew I had to have her in my life. All that time spent fighting in Vietnam, it was nothing to the fear causing me to shake when I said hello to her and asked if she remembered me."

His eyes are liquid, and he gives a nod of the head. "And the rest, as they say, is history. We lived happily ever after, at least for a time."

There is so much more there I'd like to find out about. I look to Shane, and he's staring catatonically at his plate. I'll find out more about Angie later in the week.

"Young lady, this is the best spaghetti I have had in years. Thank you so much for cooking tonight."

I blush again since I'm not sure if John Michael is being sarcastic or attempting to protect my feelings.

He makes a smacking noise with his tongue. "You Alabama girls, y'all use some different seasonings than what the girls in Georgia use." He makes the smacking noise again. "Sorta gives it a toasty taste."

Chapter 23

Going to bed in my new room, I'm worried the little girl ghost that visited me the night before will come again. I wake up disappointed she didn't.

I can be conflicted like that at times.

The thing about it is my curiosity often outstrips my common sense. In the case of the little girl ghost, I want to know her story. I want to know who she is and why she's still here. I guess in that manner, I'm a lot like my brother Dusty. I just want answers.

Where we differ is once I have the knowledge, I'm ready to drop out of the paranormal world and act like it doesn't even exist. Unfortunately, it's not as easy as turning a switch on and off. It's more like a dimmer. You can dim it down, but that doesn't mean something potent, a powerful surge, can't come through and light your whole life up again with paranormal absurdities.

I pad into the bathroom, giving a wary look at the closed door. I wash my hands and face and go to the kitchen.

It's a bit disconcerting to see that my charge, John Michael, is already up and sitting on the back porch. I open the sliding glass door. "You're up early."

He shoots me a grin. "The sun has been up for a couple hours, young lady."

I'm sure it has. "Are you hungry?"

He rubs his belly. "I think I could eat a bite."

"What do you like to eat?" I'm praying it's something like Wheaties cereal and not biscuits and gravy.

"I think I'm hankering for a boiled egg this morning and some juice."

"Okay. Give me a minute." The juice I can do, the boiled egg I'll have to YouTube.

I retreat to the kitchen as I watch a YouTube labeled "Boiling the Perfect Egg." That sounds about right. As I get a small pot out to cook his eggs, I quickly check for boxed cereal. Yep, there is none. I suppose it was too much to ask for. Honestly, I would have even eaten some Grape Nuts like Granny keeps if I found a box.

I fill a pot with water as I lament that I'm going to go hungry this morning. I pull the carton of eggs out and put two in the water for John Michael. Well, heck, when in Rome. I put two more in for myself.

As the water boils, I look out of the bay window in the kitchen. The house sits forty feet up from the lake, giving a relaxing view over the water dotted with assorted styles of boathouses. Two kids go by on jet skis.

Exhaling, I feel all the anxiety leaving my body. It's hard to be wound too tight when I'm at the lake. There is something that just opens my steam valve and lets all the pressure out.

"I hope orange juice is okay. I didn't know which one you wanted," I say as I step out onto the porch with our breakfast.

"Perfect. You read my mind."

His comment gives me a startle, but I know I didn't read his mind. I sit down next to him, hand him a bowl with two eggs, and place the salt shaker on the table.

He points over to the neighbor's yard. "Look right there. Do you see the woodpecker?"

I squint against the sun coming through the trees. "I don't."

"Wait, you will. Be patient."

If John Michael only knew patience is the one attribute I am most lacking in. I draw a deep breath and continue to watch. I see a quick flutter of movement milliseconds before I hear the rat-a-tat-tat of the woodpecker at work. I laugh. "I see him now."

John Michael chuckles. "Pete's going to be pissed. He likes to sleep in, and that woodpecker gets started pretty early."

"I thought they usually cut a nest in the spring."

"They are more active in the spring. But they do that looking for bugs, too." John Michael cuts his eyes to me with a grin. "I think that one just does it year-round though to piss off Pete."

Giggling, I peel my egg. "Well, I'd say that would about do it."

In what seems like an incredibly quick motion, John Michael has peeled his first egg, salted it, and bitten it in half. I'm still struggling with the shell. It comes off and leaves my egg badly scarred as it did not come off cleanly.

I salt my egg and stare at it. This doesn't seem like such a good idea now. Oh, what the heck. I bite the egg in half and fight back a gag. I know what egg tastes like. It's the texture that has me a little wigged out now. It takes a mighty effort, but I begin to chew and finally can swallow the egg. Next time I'll try a smaller bite.

"John Michael, a name has come up a couple of times, and I want to ask you about her."

He continues to look out over the water. "Who's that."

"Lulu."

He smiles at me. "Lucille Amber White," he says with an air of pride. He gives me a wink. "You two would have been thick as thieves. I see a lot of her in you."

John Michael's body language brightens my spirit. "How so?"

His face takes on a dreamy appearance. "She was my beautiful little tiger. When her mama would make her wear a dress, she always looked like a beautiful doll. Curly blond hair, green eyes, and just so bright. Bright as the sun like her mama."

He shakes his head while grinning. "She tied Angie in knots. You see, Lulu was a bit of a tomboy. She was happiest in a pair of shorts running around these woods with my old service backpack. Lulu would stuff it full of odd rocks, leaves, bugs, and an occasional snakeskin. Anything she thought interesting.

"She was a darn good fisherman, too. I remember she would make me take her out on the boat every weekend, and we'd fish for bass, crappie, and catfish."

He pauses, and I'm not sure if he'll continue. "She was something. One of those people who you know is going to change the world. Change it for the better."

We sit in companionable silence. A group of ducks lands, breaking the glass-like surface of the lake.

"What happened to her?" I wish I didn't have to ask, but I can't help it.

John Michael shakes his head once. "Don't know. She went out to play one day after school like she had a thousand times before. She never came home."

My heart sinks. It's impossible to imagine the horror of your child not coming home.

"For a while, I thought she might be alive." He turns to look at me, his eyes holding desperation in them. "You know? I thought she was lost. We organized search parties. This is on top of what the police were doing. But it was like she just vanished into thin air. Literally just vanished. No trace."

He exhales loudly. "Of course, my mind went to the next thing that could happen to her. I became angry, and I'm not proud of it, but I started to drink more. At the same time, Angie was cracking at the seams. It was like she lost her shine; it was a total eclipse. She'd lost her baby, too. I don't have many regrets in my life, but I do regret not being there when Angie needed me the most."

"Y'all were both hurting. It's hard to heal and help others at the same time."

"Don't you believe that!" John Michael glares at me. I find

myself leaning back from him. "I don't know who put that in your mind, but trust me. It's easier for two injured people to lean on each other than to go it alone. I did irreparable damage to our relationship. It never healed, and then three years later, as punishment, God took Angie from me. She had the sugars, and we never even knew it."

"I'm sorry."

"We reap what we sow, April. Shane's daddy Mickey, he's two years younger than Lulu. He got caught up in the crossfire. He still hasn't forgiven me, which is why we don't have much of a relationship. Still, I'm thankful every day he didn't keep my grandson away from me. He let me have that relationship. That, I'm thankful for."

"I know Shane loves you."

"I love him more." John Michael smiles. "Can I give you a bit of advice, April?"

"Sure."

"Be easy on the ones you love. You don't want them to leave you."

John Michael's simple bit of advice pokes hard at my heart. Immediately my mind goes to all the people in my life who love me. Am I easy on them? Or am I being hard?

I know the answer immediately, and I'm not pleased with it. I don't want to have regrets at the end of my life because I have pushed away people who care.

It also reminds me I have not texted Mama since the last time we talked.

Do better, April.

"I have got something for you."

His voice draws me out of my trance. "You do?"

He brings his hand out of his pocket. "Every young lady needs one of these for protection. I got this one out because it's the exact same model I gave Lulu, and like I said, you remind me of her."

John Michael hands me a bronze pocket knife. I turn it over in my hand. "A Case."

"A knife comes in handy in a lot of different situations. Also, as a last resort, defense."

Laughing, I get up. "I'll be right back. I need to get something to show you."

I retrieve my purse and, stepping back onto the porch, pull out my Ballock dagger. "A friend of mine made this for me."

John Michael holds his hand out, and I hand him the blade. "My, this one's a beauty."

"Lethal, too."

"Four-sided blade, that took some skill."

I bubble over with pride about Luca, the young juvenile delinquent I convinced a blacksmith to take under his wing recently. "Would you believe it's his first piece?"

"Unbelievable."

"And it was made from a piece of iron taken from a thirteenth-century Romanian keep."

He hands the blade back to me. "Impressive and an excellent weapon for self-defense. But a little impractical if you're trying to cut yourself free from a seat belt after an accident."

I grin. "Point taken. Thank you for the knife." I slide it into my pocket.

Chapter 24

John Michael is watching TV in the den, and I'm studying in the kitchen when my phone rings. It's Shane. "Hey, how's it going?"

"I was calling to ask you the same thing."

"Good. We had breakfast together, and he's watching TV right now."

"Okay, listen, if you want to kill some time, he likes to go out on the boat. The keys are in the drawer to the right of the stove at the very back. Don't let him see you get them."

I start to giggle as I realize the importance of keeping keys out of the hands of John Michael, whether it be boats or cars. "Yeah, that sounds like fun."

"There is a marina at the next inlet. Pop can show you where. He has an account for gas there in case y'all need to fill up anytime this week."

"Cool. How's the conference?"

"It's sort of interesting. The other reason I called is, have you taken care of getting the information about your new job to Carl."

Peaches. I knew I'd forgotten something. "I'm just waiting on Uncle Howard to send it to me. But thank you for the reminder. I need to call him and see where it's at."

"Okay, I just wanted to remind you because Carl said you

need to get it to him no later than Monday. Seeing how today's Monday."

Yeah, how about that. "I'm on it. Thank you again for the reminder."

"Least I could do since you are taking care of Pop for me. I gotta get back in. I'll talk to you later."

"Bye."

I hang up, set my phone on the counter, and stare at it as if it's a rattlesnake. I so do not want to call my uncle and ask for this favor. But in the context of getting out of a twenty-thousand-dollar judgment against me and having my wages garnished at my first job, it's a small price to pay.

As if running a sprint, I pick up the phone and dial Snow and Associates. Then everything slows down. I become self-conscious again as my anxiety builds. On the seventh ring, Howard picks up. "Snow and Associates."

"Uncle Howard, hi, this is April."

"April?"

"Your niece." Which sounds stupid as soon as I say it.

He chuckles. "I know who April is. I'm surprised you're calling. Is everything okay? What's the matter?"

John Michael's words come back to me, and I'm embarrassed. "Yes, sir. Everything's great. Except I need a little help with something."

"Oh, what's that?"

How do I explain this and not spill the beans to the Snow family that I'm unemployed? "I have this issue with my apartment. It's not what I thought it would be, and they won't let me out of my lease. I found a much better and less expensive place to live, but to get out of my lease, I need to show I have been transferred at least ninety miles away."

There is a long pause on the phone. I check to make sure the call isn't dropped. No, we're both on the line.

"I was wondering if you could send me a letter that says you've hired me."

"You need me to forge a document so you can duck out of a

legal agreement."

Well, it sounds shady when he says it like that. "Yes, sir."

I hear him exhale on the other side of the line. "I tell you what. I'll do this, but you have to promise me something in return."

Oh boy, here we go. "Yes, sir."

"I need you to promise me if anything ever goes wrong at Master, Lloyd, and Johnson, you will come home and work with me for six months before you take another position."

"Why?"

"Do you want the letter or not, April?"

"Yes, sir."

"You're asking me to do something illegal. I don't take well to forging documents given my profession. You, if anyone, should understand that. If I'm going to do this for you, I expect a big promise back. Fair?"

I had always heard my uncle was an excellent negotiator. Now I'm getting living proof of it. "Yes, sir, that's fair."

"Good, look for it in your email in the next hour. Is there anything else you need?"

I guess, in retrospect, I should have started out by buttering him up talking about his golf game. I'm feeling sort of sleazy now. "No, sir. Thank you for your help."

"Happy to oblige my niece. But, April..."

"Yes, sir."

"Don't forget your promise. You're only as good as your word."

"Yes, sir."

I hang up and realize I'm digging my hole deeper. It's only a matter of time before Howard finds out I'm working for a different firm in Atlanta, and I'll have broken my promise. It makes me uncomfortable, but I'll just have to cross that bridge when I come to it. I need his letter, and I would have promised him anything to get it.

I walk into the den to ask John Michael if he wants to go on the boat ride like Shane suggested. He's sitting in his recliner, but the TV is off. As I approach, I see his face is all screwed up, and he's pushing on his stomach.

"John Michael, are you okay?"

He looks up and nods. "Yeah, honey. I just have a little gas or something."

"You want me to go get your pain medicine?"

"No," he grunts.

"Do you want some bourbon?"

"Darn, woman. Can't you just let me be a moment?"

His words are like a slap, and I lean back. Then I become agitated. "I'm not going anywhere until you tell me what's going on. I don't know if you can figure this out, but you need help. We all need a little help from time to time, but you really need help right now. But I can't help you if you don't tell me what's going on."

He glares at me, and his nostrils flare, and I know we're about to get into it. But I'm okay with that because he's not going to talk to me that way.

"You are a spitfire, aren't you?" He laughs, but it's cut short by a wince.

I can't tell you why I do next what I decide to do. Maybe it's because I'm feeling guilty about how I have been treating my family, or perhaps because I have enjoyed John Michael's company and he can't talk when he's hurting. Most likely it's because I really could use a boat ride, but I make up my mind. "Stand up."

His brow furrows. "Can't you tell I'm in pain, woman?"

"Yes, but do as I say."

I expect him to argue further, but instead, he lets the recliner footrest down and struggles to his feet. I grab him by the elbow and steady him. "So, what now?" he says.

Stepping back, I open my arms wide. "Give me a hug."

"Ma'am?"

"You heard me. Give me a hug."

He continues to stand still, and a grin of confusion blooms across his face.

"For Pete's sake, I'm not gonna hurt you," I say as I move in and put my arms around him. His pain hits me hard in the gut, taking my breath away. I steady myself and lean into him. The heat builds between our bodies, and as his pain level becomes even more evident to me, I'm amazed he's still standing.

Once I have my breath back, I close my eyes, focus on the energy around us, and pull it in between us. Slowly, I sap away the deep pain that riddles his cells and replace it with light.

I feel his arms lock around me as he reciprocates the hug. The energy levels between us continue to grow, and finally, I know I must break from him. I push back, and he releases me.

"What was that?" he says in amazement.

"I come from an extensive line of huggers. In my family, they say there is not much a hug can't fix."

John Michael's quizzical smile makes me laugh. "I would say your family is pretty smart. But I don't know anybody in my family who hugs like that. You about gave an old man a heart attack."

"You're a cur, John Michael." I gesture toward the kitchen. "I was talking to Shane earlier, and he said it might be a fun idea to go on a boat ride. What do you think about packing a lunch and going out?"

"That sounds really good."

"Awesome. What sort of sandwich do you want?"

"Bologna and cheese," he says.

I grimace. I have not eaten bologna and cheese since middle school. Truthfully, I don't remember if I like them or not. But once I found out you can have a ham or turkey sandwich, it didn't make much sense to have bologna.

"Can you get the cooler while I make us a couple of sandwiches?"

"Sure. I'll be right back."

There is a giddy-up in his step. He looks like he is genuinely happy to be able to do something to help. That makes me feel good. When he steps out of the room, I hustle down the hallway.

I barely get the bathroom door closed and my head over the commode before I vomit. Black bile fills the toilet, and the stench is horrendous. A second wave hits, and I swear my tailbone is about to come out of my mouth when I heave. I flush the commode and sit back on my haunches, watching the black bile go down the drain. I stay in that position, wondering if I'm done being sick.

The taste in my mouth is awful, and I go to stand. As I do, another bout hits me, and my stomach grips my spine as I lurch forward and make a gosh-awful sound. One tiny drop of black liquid falls into the bowl of water and discolors it a dark purple. Standing up, I flush the commode and turn to the sink.

I'm sweating profusely now as I rinse my mouth and then splash water on my face. Then I rinse my mouth out again.

Feeling a little better but tired, I move toward the kitchen. John Michael is sitting at the counter.

"Where'd you go?"

"Just had to go to the ladies' room really quick."

"Are you okay?"

I pull down a loaf of bread and some small bags of chips. Then I gather up mayonnaise, mustard, and cheese. I roll my eyes when I see the only lunchmeat in the meat container is bologna. I have eaten it before. I suppose it won't kill me.

Taking the knife, I smear mayonnaise on one piece of bread and mustard on the other. I take a slice of cheese and am about to put it on the mustard.

"Wait a second. Is that my bologna sandwich?"

I hold the cheese in the air. "You don't like cheese?"

"I do, but you're doing it wrong."

I grin like a loon. "I am, am I?"

"Sure. Mustard goes on the bologna side, and the mayo goes on the cheese side. Everybody knows that. I like extra mayo on mine."

I do as he requests, all the time wondering if it makes a difference in how the sandwich tastes. I start to put his sandwich in a plastic bag, and he stops me again.

"You're not going to cut the crust off?"

"I can. Is that how you like it?"

"Well yeah, do you like the crust?"

I laugh nervously. "I don't not like it. But I don't really think about it."

He seems to consider that as I trim the crust off his sandwiches. "Interesting," he says.

I pack us four bottled waters and a couple packs of chips each, and put a frozen gel ice block in the cooler. "I guess we're about ready to go," I say.

The error of my ways hits me at once. I forgot to get the boat key out. "John Michael, can you go and let the boat down while I go to the restroom?"

His brow furrows. "If your stomach is bothering you, maybe we shouldn't go."

"I'll be okay."

He has a look of concern but does as I ask and heads outside. I don't like sending him down to the boathouse by himself, but I figure I can locate the key and get down there before he hurts himself.

Once he's off the deck, I open the drawer where Shane told me I'd find the key. It's because I'm trying to beat the clock, but I don't see the key. I continue digging frantically as I realize I just sent an old man with bouts of dementia to work with mechanical equipment near a lake. Not a good combination.

The silver key catches my eye at the back left of the drawer with a Post-it Note pad covering most of it. I grab it and pick up the cooler as I head out the sliding glass door. I trot in my flip-flops as quick as I can to the boathouse.

As I enter, I'm expecting to see blood or a drowned John Michael in the water. Instead, he's sitting in the driver's seat of the boat. Which has been lowered neatly into the water.

"Welcome aboard," he says.

"Move over, buddy. I'm playing skipper today," I say as I store the cooler.

He looks at me suspiciously as he changes over to the shotgun seat. "You know what you're doing?"

"Do fat babies poot?"

John Michael laughs and sits down. "Yes, they do."

We stop the boat in an alcove after we've ridden for an hour. It's still early, but I break out the food, and we both start to eat.

I quickly remember why I quit eating bologna sandwiches. It's not the worst thing in the world, and it beats going hungry, but if there are other things to eat, I won't have another for a while.

John Michael has already torn through his sandwich and is on his second bag of chips. It's good to see him eat.

Sometimes it's better not to know things. From our hug earlier today, I know John Michael isn't long for this world. Truthfully, I'm surprised he's still here. There must be some driving force to make someone endure the level of pain he's dealing with. Despite his determination and survivor spirit, it makes me nervous. I'm glad Shane will be back Friday because I really don't want to be the girl who was watching Pop when he passed.

"Shane tells me you're a lawyer," he says.

"I graduated from law school, but until I'm working as a practicing lawyer, I wouldn't call myself that."

"You'll be a great lawyer. I can see you doing really well in that role."

I pick at the remaining half of my sandwich. "I used to think that."

"Used to?"

"You know how you can start to have doubts about things. When you think you're good at something and suddenly your mind starts screaming, 'You're a fraud'?"

He tilts his head to the right. "You think you're a fraud?"

I shrug. "Sort of."

He frowns. "No. You're the furthest thing from a fraud I have met. You're a straightforward lady. You're a real "what you see is what you get" type. Or at least that's what I have experienced."

I lock eyes with him. "I appreciate that."

He raises a finger. "But I wasn't done. I think instead of being a fraud, what you're really feeling is that hole inside."

"Hole?"

He nods. "H-O-L-E. A big hole like how a doughnut has a hole."

"John Michael, I hear you, I just don't understand what you mean."

"That's all I mean. You have a big hole that needs to be filled before you're going to be okay with yourself. I don't know what's causing that hole, but it's there. But you're no fraud, April Snow."

I don't know how to respond. All I can do is smile at him.

He points at my sandwich. "Are you going to eat that?"

Chapter 25

I just got John Michael situated in his bedroom for the night when my phone rings. "How lucky am I to get two calls in one day?"

"It's only fair since I am imposing on you," Shane says.

"We actually had an enjoyable day."

"Did y'all binge watch a show on 'new flicks'?" Shane asks sarcastically.

"No, I took a friend's advice, and we had a very nice picnic lunch on the boat, and then when we got back, we took showers, and he took me out to the finest restaurant in Flowery Branch."

"You went to dinner? Where?"

"Larry's fine dining."

Shane burst into laughter, and I began to giggle too. Larry's is a "meat and three" run by another ex-military who does a decent job on the meat, but all the vegetables are straight out of a can.

However, it was delightful to see John Michael in his element. All the waitresses cut up with him, and the owner, Larry, came out and shook his hand and talked to him about politics for a bit.

"That place is awful," Shane continues.

"I have had worse," I say.

"He probably had such a big time with you. He's going to kick me to the curb."

"Funny, that's exactly what he said."

"Now that's not even funny."

"I think it's hilarious," I say with a laugh.

"Here, you're all mean, and I wanted to check in and make sure you are okay and also that you got the paperwork in on your apartment."

"Yes, it's in, and I got Carl all happy. I have to admit that's a relief for me."

"It solves one problem and throws you into another. You have to figure out where you're going to stay, girl."

"I originally thought I'd just sleep in my car for a while, but that seems awfully cramped," I blurt out without thought.

"You what?"

"I'm just joking." My ears feel hot.

"That's not funny, either."

"You don't have to get all touchy about it," I say.

"I know you have to be in early. I called Connie, and she'll be there at six in the morning."

"Okay."

"Thank you again for doing this, April. I'll see you Friday afternoon."

"Not if I see you first."

He laughs. "Good night."

While my phone is in my hand, I figure I might as well make use of it. I text Mama.

Hi, Mama. I just got in from dinner and am about to go to bed. I hope everything's going well at home. Love you.

I strip down to my panties and pull on a sleeping T-shirt. I set my alarm, turn out my light, and pull the covers up. My phone dings, and I check the message.

Thank you for the text, baby. Your daddy and I send all the love in the world. Mama.

Grinning at the customary signing of her texts, I add a heart to her message and put my phone down.

She's standing at the foot of my bed and waves her flashlight for me to follow her. I stand and look for my shoes, but I already have red Keds sneakers on. I don't remember owning a red pair.

Lulu motions again impatiently with her flashlight, and I step toward her. She makes her way out of my bedroom, and I note the large backpack she has cinched to her back. We head out through the glass door, and I'm on the deck but can't remember opening the door.

There is no time to consider that because, for a little girl, she moves quickly on her long legs. I jog to catch up with her and fall into step with her fast marching on the lake's edge. We get to the end of the inlet, and she goes down a deer trail. Thick fog blankets our steps, and more than once, I feel the squish of an invisible mud puddle under my foot.

"Where are we going?"

She doesn't answer me. She just looks over her shoulder and motions again with the flashlight. We quick-step along the state highway, and I see a couple of older homes to the right along the lake. To our left is dense woods on a gradual slope. In the distance, the hill continues to climb and becomes a small mountain. Lulu ducks off the road and heads toward the tree line.

The thickness of the undergrowth increases exponentially, and I fear I'm going to get caught in the vines and briars. Still, somehow we slide through and continue our fast pace up the mountain. We come to a small shelf toward the peak with a giant oak tree on the level space. I look up, and it must be fifty feet tall with a full plume. The sky above is an odd gray-and-yellow color, as if a tornado is coming.

I look back to the ground, and I almost miss her moving behind the big tree. I race to the back of the tree and find a rocky ledge. Lulu is climbing up the ridge, and I hesitate. It looks less than stable. The rock is sandstone and falls off the cliff as she scrambles up the incline.

My curiosity gets the best of me, and I follow her up and miraculously don't slide at all. I freeze as I watch her work between an iron grate covering a twenty-four-inch hole in the mountain slanted at a forty-five-degree angle. When she clears the grate and is on the opposite side, I move forward.

There is a tremendous ringing in my head as I near the cave entrance. I can't stand the intensity. I cover my ears.

Waking with a start, I slap my phone and try to catch my breath. Paranormal visions are rarely reliable. Sometimes, just like dreams, there are things that your subconscious has held onto during the day.

Sure, John Michael did discuss Lulu with me today, but he did not mention the cave. In fact, I didn't have a discussion with anybody about a cave, especially not a hidden cave.

This makes me think there must be a clue or some kernel of truth in the vision. I just need some help figuring out what I have seen.

Chapter 26

The doorbell rings at six o'clock sharp. An attractive woman with stark white hair and lively blue eyes holds a tray in front of me.

"Are you April?"

"Yes, ma'am. Are you Connie?"

She steps in. "I am. Would you like some biscuits and gravy?"

"Whoa, that sounds really good. But I've got to leave. Do you mind if I snag a biscuit?"

"I would be upset if you didn't."

I follow her into the kitchen and wrap a biscuit in a paper towel. "He's still not up. We had sort of a big day yesterday."

Her eyebrows arch. "Oh. Is he feeling better?"

Connie seems like she's in the know about John Michael. I should level with her. "I think he just had sort of an energy spurt. Overall, I don't think he's doing well."

She smiles. "The best we can do is keep him comfortable and show him love these last few days."

She's *really* in the know. Of course, that makes sense if they've been neighbors all this time and were good friends. There are probably few secrets between them.

"I better shove off." I walk toward the front door and stop. "Connie, do you know of any caves around here?"

She cranes her head out of the kitchen. "There are lots of caves around here. Some of the largest in the country are only an hour away."

"I mean here in the neighborhood. Specifically, any that might have been closed up at one time."

An odd expression crosses Connie's face. "There is one up at Jasper Hill." She narrows her eyes. "Why do you ask?"

"Someone at Larry's last night mentioned a cave. My brother writes ghost stories and has been asking about any caves that could be cast as spooky. I thought I might check it out for him. Could you show it to me?"

"Oh, April. I don't think anybody's been up on that mountain in fifty years. I tell you what, I'll point it out to you tonight when you get back. But really, I doubt you can even get up there anymore."

"That's a huge help. Thank you, Connie." I raise the biscuit. "And thank you for the biscuit."

"You're welcome, sweetie."

Chapter 27

The idea of solving the mystery of Lulu's disappearance dominates my thoughts while I work. It does seem like finally I may have found a beneficial use for my paranormal abilities to talk to or see ghosts. It would mean the world to John Michael if he knew what happened to Lulu. It reminds me of the young woman I found in Biloxi, Mississippi, Memory Reid.

Her mother had waited decades to find out about her daughter, and although we all like to hold out hope our loved one is alive, closure is the second-best thing. Being able to bury someone you love at least can offer the opportunity to start the healing process.

The morgue phone goes off. I answer, and the nurse tells me I have a patient over in the emergency room. Three patients are already in the morgue, but it's blissfully quiet when I open the freezer.

I take the side entrance to the emergency room and start down the hall. I have learned the different operating rooms and patient rooms now and go straight to OR number three. I smile as I step inside and see a familiar face. "Hi, Jane."

She flashes a smile. "Hi yourself, April. How have you been?"

"Pretty good. I think I'm starting to figure things out."

"Good." She continues to stare at me. Her mouth parts

slightly as if she wants to say something else.

She doesn't, so I point at the patient wrapped in the white plastic on the table. "Do we have paperwork yet?"

"Yes." She pulls a release sheet from her clipboard and hands it to me. "April, about the other day."

"What about it?"

She turns her right hand over nervously. "I just didn't want you to think … you know, think I'm crazy."

Other than my family, I prefer people not to know about my abilities. Sue me, I don't like being considered a freak. But I'm going to make an exception. "Jane, let me ask you something."

She leans back and purses her lips.

"This patient here." I look down at the sheet. "Ramirez. Do you hear his voice?"

"No."

"But that big, white dude from the other day, the one that died of sepsis, Jamie Coe. You heard him screaming, didn't you? Screaming to get the doctor that he wasn't dead."

Her eyes open wide. "How do you know? Did you hear him, too?"

"Yes. I think sometimes folks who have just died can reach out and communicate with some of us."

She points at me. "But you heard him, too?"

"Loud and clear."

"Oh, thank you, Jesus. I thought I was going crazy," she says.

"I don't know if this proves you aren't going crazy; it might just mean we're both crazy."

"I suppose that would be okay, too." She laughs. "I can always use the company. Let me give you a hand with Mr. Ramirez."

After talking to Jane about Jamie Coe, I feel bad. I had promised Jamie that I'd get his son his letter. It's not an eloquent letter, and I'm not sure how I'd react if I had a similar letter from a father who didn't show me love while he was alive.

Still, a promise is a promise, and I'd hate to cut a young boy out of the opportunity of deciding if the letter meant something to him or not.

I pull the card from my purse. I have carried it around since Sunday. I write down the rambling speech Jamie gave me on a legal pad while I play the recording.

Next, I take great care in transcribing his words to the card as legibly and neatly as possible. If a young man is going to be remembering his father ten or twenty years from now by this card, I don't want it to look messy or have a bunch of cross-outs.

Finishing, I put the card in its envelope and tuck it away in my purse. I'll have to wait until next week to deliver it since I'm taking care of John Michael. But at least I already have it done.

Chapter 28

Walking into John Michael's, I'm greeted by a heavenly smell. I make my way into the kitchen to find Connie happily working on dinner. "I had no idea this would include dinner, too."

Connie smiles. "Just a little something I'm throwing together."

"If it means John Michael and I don't have to eat my cooking tonight, bless you, you're a saint." I don't want to be rude, but I'm curious. "What is it?"

"Chicken Alfredo," she says.

Two pounds appear on each side of my buttocks. I sure hope John Michael has an appetite tonight, because if there is any extra, I'll be eating it like the greedy piglet I am. "Sounds great."

"If you'll go ahead and set the table, we'll eat now, and it should still be light enough for me to show you where the trail used to be up to the cave."

With the events of the day, I'd almost forgotten about the cave. "That would be fantastic."

John Michael comes in from the master bedroom. "What cave?"

"April was asking about the cave up on Jasper Hill."

"I have got some fond memories of that cave."

Connie glares at him. "You're probably one of the reasons they sealed it."

"Maybe," John Michael says as he strokes his stubbled chin.

Connie's pasta dishes should be outlawed. I pop the top button on my jeans and pray what I consumed doesn't expand anymore. "That was so good, Connie. Thank you."

She rises and starts to collect the dirty dishes. "I'm glad you liked it."

"Let me get the dishes when we get back. You take us to the cave before it gets dark."

She dries her hands on a hand towel. "Are you sure?"

"Yes, ma'am. Like I said, it would mean a lot to my brother."

"Okay. Let's go."

Chapter 29

I'm standing on the broken asphalt of the state highway, looking up at Jasper Mountain. The underbrush, though thick, looks much more manageable than what Connie showed me after dinner. Everything seems a little off. But the mountain's the same.

Lulu's beckoning me forward again with her flashlight. The fog is thicker tonight. There is a cold bite in the air that I hadn't noticed earlier.

In shorts and a thin T-shirt, Lulu does not seem to be affected by the cold as a shiver convulses through me. I follow her up the mountain, and again, the undergrowth and the briar bushes part ways and allow us up the hill.

I know where we're going this time, and I start around the giant oak tree and climb up the sandstone ledge. At the top, at a forty-five-degree angle, the grate closes the hole in the mountain's side. Lulu tightens her backpack straps and slides between the edge of the iron grate and the cave edge.

I step forward to follow her, but the opening is too narrow for me. She waves her flashlight again.

"I'm too big," I tell her.

She waves her flashlight frantically. I can see in her face a certain level of panic.

"I'm sorry. I won't fit."

The fog at my feet begins to thicken and swirl. Soon it is at my waist as I grab the edge of the iron grate to see if there is any way to pull it forward or push it back to make more room. I look back in Lulu's direction, and she turns into mist and melts into the fog. The fog continues to thicken until I can no longer see inside of the cave.

I grab two of the iron grate rods and shake them in frustration. "No!" It doesn't budge. Lulu is gone.

Chapter 30

Since lunch, I have been jumping to attention every time I think I hear a car in the drive. Shane said he would be coming home Friday afternoon, and he promised he would grill steaks and we would be able to eat dinner together as a family. It's pathetic that I'm this hung up on a guy I know doesn't feel the same way about me. But even if we just remain friends, I really like his company, and I have come to terms with it. If friends are all we can be, I'm okay with that.

I think it's exceptionally mature of me.

John Michael and I have had a fabulous week, especially with the help of Connie on Tuesday and Thursday. Even though he mainly conceals his pain. I'm afraid it won't be long before John Michael either must start using heavy pain medication or slips away from us entirely.

With Shane's parents being in Norfolk, I worry about him.

The door opens, startling me back to life. John Michael is rising from his chair as I come into the den, and Shane strolls in with his suitcase in tow.

"We were about to send the Marines after you, White," I say.

"I probably could've used a few armed guards at the luggage aisle," he says with a smile.

John Michael gives Shane a hug. Shane hesitates and then hugs him back. "Glad to have you home, son."

"Glad to be back. Are you hungry? Because I'm starving."

"I have got the steaks marinating like you asked."

"Good. Let me change into something more comfortable, and I'll get busy."

When he disappears into the bathroom, I jog back into the kitchen and check on my surprise. I YouTubed how to bake potatoes. Technically they have been done for an hour and a half, but I turned off the oven and left them in to stay warm. I pull out the steaks that I'm marinating in the refrigerator and put them on the counter.

I reach into the fridge to get a beer out for Shane. As I turn to put his beer on the counter, Shane is examining the steaks.

He is wearing a loose, emerald-green sleeveless T-shirt and black swim trunks that hit at mid-thigh. The sun coming in through the glass door frames him in a golden glow that causes my heart to stop as I take in the heavenly vision.

He doesn't notice me gawking as he checks the steaks. "They look good, April. I'll get the grill started."

Shane steps outside onto the deck and starts the grill. I watch curiously as he walks down to the boat dock. There he strips off his shirt and dives into the lake.

I feel voyeuristic watching him. It seems like a private moment I shouldn't be witnessing. But I can't tear my eyes away as I watch him free stroke to the center of the inlet and start back.

"Never could keep that boy out of the water. You'd swear he's half fish."

"I guess it's a good thing he's got a granddaddy with a lake house."

John Michael chuckles. "Yep. That would make him pretty fortunate."

Shane pulls himself out of the lake and slicks his hair back. His sleek, glistening muscular body is beautiful. All the times I imagined him shirtless, my imagination never did him justice.

"So, how are your potatoes?" John Michael asks.

I cut my eyes to him. He's grinning wide. I roll my eyes. "My potatoes are fine, thank you very much."

He begins to laugh in earnest and walks out onto the deck.

I come from a line of men that are true Grill Masters. My expectations are high. As I finish the last of my sirloin, I can tell you Shane could hold his own with my brothers. That's saying a lot.

For the past few days, I'd been thinking about this moment. By my way of thinking, it's the perfect time to have the discussion. Really, it isn't going to be much of a debate, as my mind is made up. It will be more of me telling them what my plans are.

"Guys, I need to tell you something." Both men give me their full attention, and I almost lose my nerve. But I need to move forward with this. "Tomorrow, I need you to help me pack—my apartment."

Both men narrow their eyes. They share a look, and Shane asks first, "Where are you moving to?"

"Here."

Shane frowns, and John Michael's eyebrows shoot up. I feel like the sun just came back up and is beating down on me because my skin feels like it's a hundred and ten degrees, and I'm starting to sweat.

"Are you serious?" Shane asks.

"Ha-ha. Too funny. I'm seventy-six years old, and it's the first time in my life I have a girlfriend move in with me," John Michael says.

"April." Shane's frown ruins his handsome face.

"It just makes sense. I'm not going to have a place to live in a couple weeks. You can't be running up here all the time because you work more hours than I do, and John Michael can use the company. I'm not saying it's forever, but for right now,

I think it makes sense for all three of us."

"Well, I for one am in," John Michael says.

Shane holds his hand up toward his grandfather. "I'm not concerned about us. I want to make sure this doesn't derail what you're trying to do in your life."

"I don't see that it does. And if it ever did, I'd let you know."

Shane's quiet, and I can tell he's running all the contingency plans through his mind. All the ways this arrangement could be helpful for everybody and all the ways it could be a total disaster. I have already done the same analysis in my own mind.

"Okay. We'll move your stuff into the garage tomorrow. But only if you promise me that if you ever need to leave, you let me know. I don't want you to ever feel obligated."

"Fair." But as Shane and John Michael have become my Atlanta family, with family come certain obligations.

Chapter 31

It's Tuesday afternoon, and I'm on top of the world. It's three o'clock, and my shift is ending. I'll be headed home to my new lake house.

Shane and I worked all day yesterday to clear out my apartment and store everything in the garage at John Michael's. It's a relief to know no matter how long it takes, two months or two years, I have the means to fulfill my dream of working in Atlanta's legal scene.

Would it complete my fantasy to also have Shane White in love with me? Yes. But my cup is three-quarters full, so who am I to complain. Besides, who knows, given enough time, he might realize the error of his ways and fall madly in love with me.

In the last two weeks, I have been checking off the boxes of things that need to be accomplished in April's life for things to calm down. I'm down to the last few items, and I think, *when better than now to take care of one of them?* I enter the address into the GPS app on my phone.

Perfect, it's only a fifteen-minute drive.

I poke my head into Janet's office. "I'm leaving now."

"Okay, honey. We'll see you Thursday."

"Yes, ma'am. Have a good night."

As I get into my car, I wonder if I'm doing the right thing.

Probably not. I have concluded that if it were me, I wouldn't want the letter from a dad who didn't care enough about me to come by and be in my life. But like I concluded before, it's not my decision. And I should leave it up to Jamie's son, David.

Driving out to their home, I wonder what the mother, Amanda Baker, is like. If she is a soft-spoken woman who's been subjected to an unbelievably selfish man? Or is she a hard, cold woman who holds resentment toward Jamie?

The homes in the neighborhood are duplexes. About half of the yards are well-maintained, the other half so poorly taken care of that I'm not sure the homes are occupied. I pull into the driveway of the unit with the correct address on the mailbox. There is an old Dodge Journey in the driveway that could use a paint job.

I take a deep breath, grab my purse, and walk up to the door. I hurry and press the doorbell before I lose my nerve.

My patience runs thin, and I press the doorbell again after half a minute wait. I hear an indistinct hollering from inside the house.

The door is yanked open, and a woman my height but fifty pounds heavier is glaring at me. Her long, chestnut-brown hair looks like it hasn't been combed in days, and her mouth is set in a snarl. "We don't want any."

"I'm not here selling, ma'am." I reach into my purse. "I'm here to give you something..."

"I don't want your free samples, either." She produces a cigarette from behind her ear, and a lighter is in her right hand. She lights the cigarette and takes an immediate long drag.

I hold the envelope out to her. "No, ma'am, it's not a sample. It's a card for David from his daddy, Jamie Coe..."

Her face twists into a knot. "Jamie."

"Your son's daddy."

She shakes her head from side to side. "I know who he is. Maybe you didn't know, but he's been dead for a week."

I shake the envelope. "Yes, ma'am, and he had a letter to his son in his pocket. It was messed up, so I copied it to a card."

She takes the card from me, pulls the cigarette from her mouth, and spits to the side as if she had a bit of tobacco on her lip. "This letter's from Jamie?"

"Yes, ma'am."

"For Davey."

"Yes, ma'am." She's a little slow on the uptake.

She grins. "Let me show you what I think of that, Missy." She holds the letter up and places her lighter under it. As the card begins to burn, she says, "And I hope he's burning just like this card."

At least I have my answer. Amanda's on the bitter, vengeful team. "Sorry I bothered you, ma'am."

"Oh, I bet you are," she says to my back as I walk to my car.

Chapter 32

My Case knife is lying in the dirt in front of me. I can't reach it. I have been looking at it for what seems like an eternity. But no matter how much I try, I can't pick it up now that I dropped it.

I wake up full of excitement. I have the house to myself, and I have been planning this day for over a week now. Shane has taken John Michael in for his monthly examination, and they won't be back until after lunch.

Pulling on a pair of jeans and a long-sleeved T-shirt, I visualize the trail from my dreams. Today I'll confirm if they have any merit or are just troubling dreams from living in an unfamiliar environment.

My plan is to head straight to my car, but I stop at the room across the hall. I place my hand on the doorknob and twist. It's not locked, and the door opens easily for me.

Oddly, there is no paranormal signature now. I am prepared for a surge, but there is nothing.

If the room I have been staying in feels like a boy's room, this one is feminine. I grin, feminine with a healthy dose of spunk.

As I suspected, it's Lulu's room. The contents are covered in years' worth of dust, and I wonder when the window was last opened. What at one time started out as a shrine to their daughter has turned into an empty crypt.

I walk over to the small gray desk that I believe may have been cream-colored forty years earlier. On it is a five-by-seven picture frame. I lift it and wipe the dust away.

John Michael isn't kidding. If the ten-year-old Lulu would appear today, I'd beg her to play the part of my Mini-Me this Halloween.

When I get to Jasper Mountain, I pull my Prius over to the side of the road. As an extra precaution, because I have an odd feeling, I leave a note in the seat explaining that I'm going to the abandoned cave.

There is no explanation why I believe the note is necessary. I have come to learn that if something odd like that crosses my mind, it's best to go ahead and go with the flow rather than apply logic.

Going up the mountain is a totally different adventure in real life than in my dream. The undergrowth is brutal, and there are vines everywhere that catch hold of my hair and shoulders, preventing me from moving forward. It takes an hour to climb the hundred-yard slope, and I never do find a path.

Coming out of the woods, I catch sight of the enormous oak tree on the shelf, so different from the tall pines and squatty cedars that dominate the rocky hillside. My pulse quickens, and I begin to sweat profusely. It's more to do with my nerves than the oppressive heat.

I march around the oak tree and start up the sandstone ledge with purpose, hurrying before I lose my nerve. Slipping down the ridge, I try to stop my fall with my hands. I end up cutting my palms bad enough for them to bleed. I dust myself off and try a second time to scale the broken rock cliff. I slide off again, but this time I turn and come down on my butt, slicing a hole in the thigh of my jeans.

If nothing else, I'm persistent. I try a third time, and I make it up the ledge. When I do, I almost wish I hadn't. My stomach rolls over as I look at the iron grate set into the cave mouth that looks more like a gully wash than a cave entrance. It's not much of an opening. I stare at it for a good while before I get the nerve to touch it. When I do, I try my luck by pulling on it. It isn't going to be that easy. It doesn't budge.

I keep looking at the edge of it. I don't understand how even a small girl could've slipped through it. Again, though, maybe that's just the fallacy of the dream.

At this stage, it's sort of like I came, I saw, I left. Because I have no way of getting into the cave.

An idea comes to me, and I pull my Case knife out of my purse. I open it up and stick the point into the large steel lock with fifty years of rust on it. I have got no particular plan, and I just jiggle the knife back and forth.

When the clasp falls into my hand, it takes me a second to realize it's open. I'm shocked.

I pull the padlock off and open the grate. Now I wish I'd brought a flashlight. At least I have my phone.

First, I hang my legs in the opening. As my legs stretch into the hole, my toe finds no rock or floor. I continue to reach with my foot. Losing my grip, I slip into the hole. It is only another foot and a half drop, but I feel my left ankle give as I land funny.

That smarts.

I'm in a round room that's ten feet by ten feet with an eight-foot ceiling. There's only one trail, and it leads further back into the mountain. I start in that direction.

I don't have a clue what I'm doing or where I'm going. At this point, I'm just hoping through blind luck to figure out this mystery. To determine if the dreams meant anything at all.

The farther I go into the cave, the more I start thinking all I saw in my dreams were some of the fun Lulu had. The things that stick and leave high-energy imprints are things that really scare you or things that bring you joy. I can see where, if a young girl liked to explore, going into an abandoned cave would leave a high energy signature on her spirit.

Disappointingly, the cave ends. I check to the left and the right, but it's just a stone wall with an exceedingly small drain-off crack to the left. There is no way to continue forward. Disheartened, I turn around and start my way back.

I should have known. I was foolish to think I'd be able to solve this mystery easily. They've had police officers, family, and friends looking for her for decades.

My love for John Michael gave me the grand illusion that I would figure this out. I feel like it would be easier for him to pass if he knows what happened to Lulu.

Sunlight pours in from the entrance a few feet ahead of me. It's not going to be easy pulling myself up and out of this eight-foot ceiling, but I think I might be able to use a large boulder just to the right as a stepping stone.

I see a hole in the cave wall I didn't notice earlier in my peripheral vision on my left. It's small, only about twelve inches around. Still, I wonder if it might have an opening to a different cave area.

I climb up the cave wall until I can look in the opening. Looking through, I see there is a thin, narrow shelf, and then the cave opens further. I pull myself halfway through the gap between the stones.

Hanging over the ledge, I shine my phone's blue light. I'm trying to see how far of a drop there is before there is a floor.

My light catches a reflection. I redirect my phone light back in that direction and stare for the longest time. There is an open Case knife on the sandy floor some twelve feet down.

My body tenses as I try to process the current information.

At the very least, that means Lulu was here. That doesn't mean something happened to her here, though. She could have lost her knife weeks before she disappeared.

If I can't give John Michael Lulu, I can give him her knife. I know it's not the same. And it might even be more problematic than helpful. But I have a burning desire to retrieve her knife for him.

I pull myself out onto the ledge. The only way forward that I see is balancing myself between two large boulders that taper to the ground. I don't like how it looks, so I shine my flashlight for an alternate path down. I see the faded, army-green fabric wedged in a crevice next to ivory sticks.

For an eternity, I stare at the small green fabric and the ivory formation. My mind doesn't want to compute what I am looking at, and I allow my eyes time to discern the item multiple times.

Steeling myself for the worst, I lean out further with the light. I see two dusty, red sneaker toes.

Reflexively, I collapse into a sitting position on the ledge. I struggle to catch my breath. I'm so numb with shock I can't even cry.

The realization crashes over me—that poor, poor baby. I have found Lulu.

How dreadfully horrible. How long did Lulu hang by her beloved backpack before she finally died of dehydration? How tragically terrifying.

I'm so crushed I don't think I will ever be able to move. I may stay here and perish with her from heartbreak.

What did you expect to find, April?

I don't know, but not this. An accident, a fall, and a broken neck. Not a little girl alone in the dark.

John Michael can't know what happened to Lulu. I can't tell him. If he knew that his daughter died emulating his wartime cave prowess, it would cause him more pain than the cancer eating his insides.

I'll carry this secret to my grave.

Now, if I can stop hyperventilating and negotiate my way out of the tunnel, I'll head home. Nobody ever must know besides me.

The sandy loam floor illuminates. Lulu comes from around a boulder. She favors me with a wide, toothy smile as she waves excitedly to me while leaping up and down. Her wide eyes sparkle with an unnatural fluorescent green in the darkness.

Oh, sweet baby. My body convulses with gut-wrenching sobs as I begin to cry.

Chapter 33

I hold John Michael's hand during Lulu's ceremony. It's been a stressful week getting to this point. At times, I have been concerned that John Michael wouldn't see his baby girl laid to rest.

Up for reelection this fall, the local district attorney wants Lulu's death investigated as a homicide. He's stoked local parents' fear that there may be a child killer in their community. Given how I found Lulu, I know it's preposterous. Still, the district attorney had requested Lulu's burial be delayed by up to a year while they complete their investigation.

Shane tells me if not for Dr. Hamlin's intervention, Lulu would not be able to be released for burial. He tells me Janet has contacts at both the medical examiners and the state attorney general. Who knew she had that sort of pull?

Moral support and comfort are not the only reason I'm holding John Michael's hand. I want him to be present today for what he has wanted to do for so many years. The low-grade heat between our palms, I hope, will keep his pain at bay long enough for him to appreciate this moment. The outpouring of love from the community for his little girl, who seems to have captured the hearts and imagination of the Flowery Branch community, is tremendous.

Lulu, for one, is enjoying herself. Her smile is intoxicating as she strolls from the preacher's podium back to her closed casket adorned with a heap of sunflowers. She runs a finger along the brown center of one of the enormous flowers then looks up. Her green eyes lock with mine from a distance, and her arm shoots into the air with a wave. I raise my left hand chest high and wave back, earning a toothy smile.

She sits down in front of her casket and pulls her red Keds under her long, thin legs. She tilts her head back as she continues to listen to the pastor, and she shines. She shines with the brightness of a tiny star that has landed on the wooden floor of that old chapel. Her light is so bright I must squint my eyes so I'm not blinded. Tears stream down my cheeks from the sight of her beauty.

"I can feel her," John Michael says at my side.

"She's here," I choke as my voice cracks.

"My beautiful little tiger."

Chapter 34

I have only managed to kick off my pumps. I'm sprawled out on Shane's daddy's childhood bed, contemplating the complexities of life. It is not a good topic for a mentally drained mind and a body that has temporarily taken on illness to help a friend.

Still, I think about the brightness that the world missed out on because of one misstep on a rock forty years earlier. How a brother can't adjust his schedule to see his sister buried and to comfort his father, no matter what has transpired between them in the past. Selfishly, I wonder how someone can be so in love with a person and not love them back.

The world just seems whacked to me.

I turn to the knock at my door. "April?"

Shane looks ten years older today. It's not the suit and tie. It's the stress in his face.

"Yes."

He squints. "Pop is ready for bed, but he says he needs to talk to you. Alone."

I'm bone-tired, and I don't have anything else to give. But I don't even consider telling Shane to tell John Michael I'll talk to him in the morning. "Okay."

I pass by Shane in the doorway and pad through the kitchen into the master bedroom. I enter John Michael's room, and at first, I think he's asleep. As I move over to his bed, his eyes, hooded, open.

"She's gone."

I sit down at the edge of his bed and nod my head. "Yeah."

"She would have loved all the sunflowers."

"Connie did a beautiful job with them."

His breath catches. "Will she come back?"

A tear rolls down my cheek. "I don't think so."

"I miss her already."

"I know you do." I laugh through my tears and tap him on the arm. "Don't be so stingy. Let her visit with Angie for a while now."

His eyes close, and he grins. Then he grimaces and grunts in pain. I reach out and grab his hand. He pulls it away. "Don't do that. I know it makes you sick, and I won't have it."

Exhaling, I put my hand on top of his. "I won't."

"All this time, I was waiting, holding on because I thought she was waiting for me to find her." His lids open, and he locks his blue eyes on me. "But all along, it was you she was waiting on."

"John Michael, if you hadn't waited, you wouldn't have been here for me, and I wouldn't have been here for Lulu."

He smiles and closes his eyes. "I like that. I like that a lot."

I watch him as his face relaxes. His breathing, shallow but steady, tells me he's asleep. He had a big important day.

I pull the sheets up to his chest, kiss him on the forehead, and then step out of the master bedroom.

Shane is at the counter. "Is he okay?"

"He's tired and sleeping."

"I think I'm gonna sleep on the chair in his room tonight. Just in case he needs something."

If I were not so tired, the anxiety on Shane's face would break my heart. Instead, I walk over to him and pull him into an embrace. While I hold him, I whisper into his ear, "You're a good man, Shane White." I pat him on the back and break our embrace.

My bed seems a mile away.

Chapter 35

I found the prettiest little lake just outside of Atlanta. It's twenty acres with a beautifully maintained pea gravel walkway around it. Even though it's the middle of the summer, there are beautiful flower beds complete with tulips, crocuses, and large rose blossoms. Planted on the pea gravel's outside perimeter are fragrant magnolia trees and gardenia bushes in full bloom. Just standing and smelling the fragrance in the air has a calming effect on me. Still, it will also be a beautiful place to exercise while enjoying the swans on the lake.

Unlike the oppressive heat in the rest of Atlanta, despite the sun being directly overhead, the weather is pleasant. I'm wearing shorts, a light T-shirt, and red sneakers. Why am I surprised Atlanta has a hidden gems like this? I'm so glad I stumbled upon this Eden.

John Michael, having passed, makes the dynamic of the lake house dramatically different now. When he was alive, I had a reason to be at the lake house besides just needing shelter, and I had company. Yes, it's the first time in my life I had a roommate, and who knew, I like it.

Now that he's gone, the situation has changed. Most nights, I'm at the lake house by myself. Shane comes up and uses it on the weekend, but since we're only friends and certain parts of my anatomy don't want to accept that, let's just say his visits are frustrating.

Before too long, I need to sit down and really rethink the trajectory of my life. I have thought about heading home a few times instead of playing this game of Atlanta against April.

Coming around the corner, I smile at a family sitting under a giant oak tree on a park bench and sharing a picnic lunch. I don't know why. They don't resemble my family, but they remind me of home. My family will often congregate on the back porch of the lake house or in the kitchen and enjoy a huge meal together.

It doesn't seem possible, but after seven years, it's like suddenly April May Snow is getting a case of homesickness. Talk about delayed reactions.

The family looks familiar, and I stare a little too long when the father looks up and locks his blue eyes with my stare. He gestures for me to come over. "Come on, April. We've always got plenty to share."

Having grown up in the South, I don't consider it odd that someone extends hospitality to a stranger. But how does he know my name?

My curiosity will be the death of me. Even though my common sense tells me to leg it back to my car and drive away, I walk toward the family.

As I approach their table, I can see their spread: bologna sandwiches and hard-boiled eggs. I look up in confusion, and the little girl turns toward me and pats the seat next to her. Her eyes are a brilliant shade of green. "Can't you stay, April?"

"No honey, April's only visiting."

The little girl frowns, and the dad adds, "She needs to fill her doughnut hole first, Lulu."

A creepy sensation begins to tickle across my skin. Something is not quite right here. The man approaches me with something in his hand, and all I can think is I need to run.

He holds out his hand. "Have you figured out what fills in your doughnut hole yet, April?"

"No, sir," I whisper.

He smiles, and I realize it's a young John Michael. "Look around you. You're making it more complicated than what it is, dear."

He holds the doughnut out toward me. It's a chocolate cruller. That's not fair. I really like those, and some comfort food would be welcome now. I reach out to take the doughnut from him, and as the stiff sugar frosting touches the tips of my fingers, a male scream reverberates in my head.

My eyes fly open, and I realize I'm in bed. I stay frozen under my sheets, wondering what I heard, and then it happens again. Throwing back my covers, I run out of my room. I hear the sob of pain again and run in the kitchen's direction. I realize it's Shane, and I burst into the master bedroom where he spent last night. I skid to a stop on my bare feet.

He's sitting on the edge of the bed, holding John Michael in his arms. John Michael's lips are purple, and it's obvious he's been gone for some time now. I look down, and I'm still in the skirt and blouse I wore last night to Lulu's funeral.

Chapter 36

Even though I prepared the master bedroom for them, Shane's parents, Mickey and Rhonda White, refused to stay at the lake home the two nights they were in Atlanta.

It is an odd family structure to witness, as Mickey and Rhonda obviously love their son as much as John Michael loved Shane. It must have been difficult for Shane to navigate the relationships with the people he loves all these years.

After the initial shock of John Michael's death, Shane pulls it together as we prepare for the funeral. Unlike Lulu's service, where the entire community was involved, John Michael's is a more straightforward affair. A few remaining coworkers from Ford, people from the neighborhood, and a couple surviving Marines attended.

Plus, John Michael, unlike Lulu, is not at his own funeral. But I had advance notice of where John Michael is, and I'm happy for him.

The ride shows up to take home the last Marine, who looks to be approaching eighty. When he leaves the lake house, I go into the kitchen to clean the dishes.

Shane comes in and starts helping.

"I've got this, Shane."

"No, I want to help. I think it'll take my mind off things."

I shrug my shoulders as I continue rinsing a platter. "Okay."

He brings a tray over next to me and sets it down. I look at him out of the corner of my eye. He's not okay.

"I can't believe he's gone."

I dry my hands. "Be happy for him; he's not in pain anymore. Maybe he is with your grandma and aunt, too. You know that would make him happy."

"But I'm all by myself now."

"I beg to differ with you." I put the towel down. "You have two parents who love you very much. That means a lot."

I can say that with a forcefulness that I have never been able to say it with before. In the last few days, I have been contemplating John Michael's question—what fills April's doughnut hole.

You know I have concluded the answer to that is a little different for everybody. And we all must figure it out on our own. But I have a sneaking suspicion that part of what fills April's doughnut hole is her family. I understand my center filling may end up being something funky like rhubarb jelly. Still, I think in the end, it may be better to have an odd filling than a hole where your heart should be in your chest.

Again, I'm not positive. I have been giving it some thought, and I think I might need to go back and find out for sure. Who knows, it might turn out that's not it at all. But I need to take the time to understand.

A tear rolls down Shane's cheek. "It's like I can't breathe without him."

He reminds me of a ten-year-old boy who just found out his puppy died. I can't help myself, and I pull him into an embrace. "I know. It'll get better."

His head comes off my shoulder, and as I feel his ear slide by mine, I think he's going to ask me a question. His warm lips press against mine, sending electrical tingles from my lips to my scalp and chest. I'm startled. Then every ounce of energy lights me up as I return his kiss. His tongue touches mine, and my world changes as heat flows through my body and my knees go weak. I never knew a kiss could feel like this!

He breaks the kiss. I don't want to open my eyes. Slowly, I do. He's looking at me with an expression of horror on his face.

"I'm sorry, April. I didn't mean to do that."

The hole in my heart just got bigger. I wish Shane had just slammed his hand into my chest and pulled my heart out. It couldn't be any more painful.

"Ah, people get emotional at times like this. It doesn't mean anything." I turn back to washing the dishes. "However, it does bring up a topic. I didn't want to bring it up with you until after today. But since we're here. I want to ask a favor."

"Name it."

I turn and face him. "I want you to let me borrow John Michael's truck and help me pack tomorrow. I need to go back to Guntersville."

His facial expression screws up. "No, April. Just because Pop is gone doesn't mean you have to leave. You can still make it here in Atlanta."

I shrug. "I'm not sure it's what I want anymore. I just want to go home for a while and figure things out first."

"Are you sure about this?"

"I am. I have been thinking about it for a few days now. I'm ready to swim with the current for a while and not fight it."

Shane raises his eyebrows, then tucks his chin. "Wow. Those words have come back to haunt me."

"It's good advice, and I trust you enough as a friend to take your advice."

"I understand. But I'm not going to kid you. I'll miss you."

Not like I want you to, buddy. "I'll miss you, too."

Chapter 37

Shane was sweet enough to be at U-Haul when they first opened to rent me a trailer for John Michael's truck. By lunchtime, we have it packed, and I shower to lie down for a nap. I figure tomorrow will be a taxing day between the drive and explaining to my family what transpired in Atlanta the last few weeks.

I wake up to the delicious smell of an Italian bistro. Half asleep, I find my way into the kitchen, where Shane is at the stove.

"I have already put in my resignation, White. You can't cook your way out of my leaving."

"Baby, I would never hold you down. This is a celebration dinner."

I walk closer to the stove. "What is it?"

He flashes me a grin. "Alabama toasty marinara."

"Please say it ain't so." I laugh.

He hands me a half-full tumbler of bourbon. I feel all the "friend" love a girl can stand. "Just to let you know what's on tap tonight … spaghetti, garlic toast, bourbon, and I found the nineteen seventy-eight version of *Dawn of the Dead* on 'new flicks.'"

"Shane White, you know how to spoil a girl." I lift my tumbler, and he taps his glass to mine.

I take a long sip of the smooth liquor. Whenever I taste bourbon, I'll think of Atlanta.

The End

You'll never miss an April May Snow release.
When you join the reader's club!

www.mscottswanson.com

Would you like to continue the journey with April? You can learn how she rebounds in her hometown of Guntersville in the **Foolish** novel series.

Click to continue reading

The *Foolish* Series

Foolish Aspirations

Foolish Beliefs

Foolish Cravings

Foolish Desires

Foolish Expectations

Foolish Fantasies

M. Scott lives outside of Nashville, Tennessee, with his wife and two guard chihuahuas. When he's not writing, he's cooking or taking long walks to smooth out plot lines for the next April May Snow adventure.

Dear Reader,

Thank you for reading April's story. You make her adventures possible. Without you, there would be no point in creating her story.

I'd like to encourage you to post a review on Amazon. A favorable critique from you is a powerful way to support authors you enjoy. It allows our books to be found by additional readers, and frankly, motivates us to continue to produce books. This is especially true for your independents.

Once again, thank you for the support. You are the magic that breathes life into these characters.

M. Scott Swanson

The best way to stay in touch is to join the reader's club!

www.mscottswanson.com

Other ways to stay in touch are:

Like on Amazon

Like on Facebook

Like on Goodreads

You can also reach me at mscottswanson@gmail.com.

I hope your life is filled with
magic and LOVE!

Made in the USA
Middletown, DE
21 February 2023

25284480R00125